Lembas for the Soul

Nominated for:
Best Tolkien-Themed
book of 2005 by
theOneRing.net

Lembas for the Soul

How
The Lord of the Rings
Enriches Everyday Life

Catherine Kohman

Lembas For the Soul:
How *The Lord of the Rings* Enriches Everyday Life

ISBN-10: 0-615-61317-9
ISBN-13: 978-0615613178

All inquiries should be sent to info@whitetreepress.com or visit us on the web at whitetreepress.com.

White Tree Press

Lembas For the Soul

We gratefully acknowledge the cover design work and interior drawings of Dana Tonello. Copyright © Loredana (Dana) Tonello, T/A "Design by Danat'ello".
E-mail: **danatello@snowboard.com**

"Mirror of Galadriel" – aquarelle pencil/Photoshop. Copyright © 2005 Loredana (Dana) Tonello. Dana's wonderful artwork can be seen on pages 72, 93 and 141.

A special thank you to Catharine Mallard whose beautiful interior artwork can be seen on pages 4, 6, 9, 41, 112 and 155.

White Tree Press WhiteTreePress.com

Lembas for the Soul

Dedication

Dedicated first and foremost to Professor John Ronald Reuel Tolkien: you have our everlasting gratitude for giving us your brilliant "sub-creation",
The Lord of the Rings

And to Peter Jackson, Fran Walsh, Philippa Boyens and all of the cast and crew of *The Lord of the Rings* films: a multitude of thanks for bringing the world of Middle-earth and its people to life in such breath-taking detail, and for honoring the spirit of Professor Tolkien's masterwork.

Table of Contents

Lembas for the Soul

The Fellowship of Ringers

Welcome to the Hall of Fire

Tales from the Green Dragon

The Road Goes Ever On

Smaug

Acknowledgments

This book could not have been written without the contributions of *Lord of the Rings* fans from across the world. It has been my privilege to collect their stories and share them with the rest of the Ringer community.

This project would have never gotten off the ground without the technical expertise, fine eye and attention to detail of my webmaster, Sarah Marshall, and her husband Terry Roberts, at www.showmewebworks.com. They took my dreams and morphed them into the lovely *White Tree Press* site. I shall plant a sapling of The White Tree in their honor.

Two *LOTR* artists have contributed their beautiful work to the project: Catharine Mallard of *The Darkling Woods Gallery*, and Dana Tonello of *Danat'ello Designs*. Not only are they gifted artists, but talented writers as well. Many blessings upon your future creative endeavors.

Another thank you to Bonnie Marlweski-Probert of *Whitehall Publishing* for gently nudging me along to get the whole work pulled together in time.

Heart-felt thanks to my husband, family and friends for their ongoing love and support, and to my sweet Elf hound, Lexie, for the hours of quiet companionship while I toiled away at the computer. A star surely lights the heavens in your honor.

Finally, I owe a great debt of gratitude to the other members of *The Sisterhood of the Ring*: Julie Sobchack, Barbara Cockrell and Carolyn Ceron. I couldn't have finished the book without your editorial input, your knowledge of the esoterica of Middle-earth, your unflagging encouragement and especially, all of the laughter. I raise a glass in salute to you, *mellyn nin*, the fairest and brightest of women.

Catherine Kohman, 2005

Goldberry

Lembas for the Soul

Introduction

I was born to be a hobbit. My birthday falls on September 22, just like Frodo's and Bilbo's. Frodo and I both had grandmothers (in my case, a *great*-grandmother) whose last name was Bolger, a well-known name in the Shire. So you can reasonably say I have hobbit blood—probably Took by all inclinations—running through my veins.

When at age fifteen I read *The Hobbit* and *The Lord of the Rings*, the books had a profound effect on me. While journeying in Middle-earth I felt a curious sense of homecoming; I'd found the landscape where my soul most wanted to wander. Posters of The Hill and Tolkien calendars hung on the walls of my room, and I wrote my first real piece of fiction, a story about a pair of Elves making a pilgrimage to Lothlorien before taking one of the last grey ships to Valinor. This was long before anyone had even invented the term "fan fiction."

Since then, I've discovered my experience is commonplace among *LOTR* fans. Loath to leave Middle-earth, we continue to explore it, whether by annual readings of the books, writing fan fiction, learning Elvish, creating works of art, repeatedly watching the *LOTR* films, attending fan "moots" or discussing all aspects of Middle-earth with online friends. People who aren't *LOTR* fans don't understand this compulsion. They dismiss *The Lord of the Rings* as a "mere fairy tale". *They just don't get it.*

I recently attended *Tolkien 2005*, a 50th anniversary celebration of *The Lord of the Rings*, held by The Tolkien Society in Birmingham, England. Martin Barker, a professor at the University of Wales at Aberystwyth, gave a presentation on his research based on over 24,000 questionnaires Ringers filled out online after the release of *The Return of the King* film in 2003. (His research will be published in a book entitled *Watching The Lord of the Rings* sometime in 2006.) I thought the most interesting finding was that the people who enjoyed the films the most were those who had read the book multiple times and who saw the tale as a spiritual journey.

Lembas for the Soul

A spiritual journey. Not escapist fiction or simple entertainment, but rather a journey of the soul. As soon as I heard that comment, all the pieces I'd been trying to sort out in my mind fell into place. It explained why so many of us have embraced *The Lord of the Rings* as a source of inspiration and illumination, and why we continue to read it every year or watch the films over and over without ever tiring of them. We aren't really geeks who need to "get a life"; we are in many ways the Enlightened Ones.

We have walked in the Fellowship's shoes so often we could probably make the journey south to Minas Tirith or Mordor without even a map. When the real world is too harsh, too bleak or demanding of us, we can turn to *LOTR* and see how our beloved heroes of Middle-earth find the courage to go on despite overwhelming odds, how they continue to have hope in the darkest of times. This is especially true for some *LOTR* fans whose experiences are included in this book. A dear friend of mine recently shared with me a pertinent quote from the scholar Roger Scruton, which often comes to mind these days: "The consolation of imaginary things is not imaginary consolation."

Yet you will find in reading the fans' stories in this volume that *LOTR* is much more than a source of comfort. For some fans *The Lord of the Rings* acts as a Muse, freeing them to explore their own creativity. For others, their love of *LOTR* has compelled them to seek out like-minded folk and they've formed strong friendships that span the globe. Some Ringers have found that *LOTR* inspires them to leave their comfy "hobbit holes" to seek new vistas and adventures of their own. For them, the open road still beckons. Other fans are simply happy to share the sheer joy and wonderment of *The Lord of the Rings* in all its forms.

Whether the stories included in *Lembas for the Soul* make you laugh or bring you to tears, you will likely find something of your own *Lord of the Rings* journey within these pages.

May the blessing of Elves and Men and all Free Folk go with you! *Namarië*!

Catherine Kohman, 2005

Iorhael

A Long Awaited Party

A Flame Re-kindled

"Have you heard about *The Lord of the Rings*?" Brad asked when he saw me passing his office door.

"Heard what?" I leaned through the doorway. Brad, the branch manager of my library, and I had both been *LOTR* fans since our youth. In fact, reading *The Lord of the Rings* aloud together had been a part of his courtship of his wife. She'd even recently designed the costumes for a theater production of *The Hobbit*.

"They're going to make a live-action version of *The Lord of the Rings*."

"*What*?" A sudden spurt of excitement made me straighten. "Are you sure?"

He nodded. "Some guy named Peter Jackson from New Zealand is directing it."

"Really?" A dubious note crept into my tone. Surely, if anyone was going to take on a live-action production of *LOTR* and make it work, it should have been Spielberg or Lucas. "I've never heard of him."

"He directed *Heavenly Creatures*."

"Oh, right." I *had* heard of that film, which had gotten some good reviews and quite a bit of press. And weren't *Hercules* and *Xena* filmed in New Zealand? At least the landscape had possibilities.

I was curious about the film, but Brad and I didn't really discuss it much after that. I'd been one of those geeks who read *LOTR* almost every year until I lost my boxed set of Ballantine paperbacks — the ones with the mutant pink covers — in a cross-country move. About five years went by before I missed the books enough to finally ask for *The Lord of the Rings* for my birthday.

Lembas for the Soul

My husband gave me the boxed set with covers by Alan Lee, although he grumbled a bit at the price. I didn't care — I felt better knowing I could now go to the shelf any time and step back into Middle-earth.

While Weta Workshop was creating thousands of prosthetic hobbit feet and the Fellowship was trekking up to the Pass of Caradhras, I was baking in the high desert, then driving across the vast emptiness of the Great Plains. This time that restless Took blood had brought my family and I to the rolling oak woodlands of Missouri. Between the move and beginning a new library job, I didn't have much time for reading.

Then one day, as I sat in a darkened theater, a fanfare of stirring music began, and Gandalf strode over the rise. No moment of hesitation, wondering who that was — it was Gandalf as I'd always imagined him. And behind Gandalf, his bright eyes ever watchful, came my favorite member of the Fellowship, and this time the reality was far better than my imagination. Ever since I'd first read *LOTR*, I'd had a profound desire for Elves. For all too brief a moment I saw *my* Legolas, a perfect vision of elven grace and beauty, then he was gone. As each member of the Fellowship crossed the screen, I knew instantly who they were. Stout-hearted Gimli, my dear Frodo, the mischief makers, Merry and Pippin, faithful Sam and Bill the pony, a grim Boromir, and looking every bit the disreputable Ranger, Aragorn. I burst into wild applause, startling everyone around me, but I didn't care. I'd seen enough. If the rest of the films held true to that vivid vision of the Fellowship, I knew I would not be disappointed.

After seeing the trailer, I did some online exploration and came across *theOneRing.net*. I read bits and pieces of *LOTR* news, but didn't visit TORn regularly. Then it was Opening Day of *The Fellowship of the Ring*. I knew nothing about line parties — I barely managed to get off work early enough that day to catch the 4:30 showing. I could only find a seat at the end of a row. But when the two women next to me offered me some of their popcorn because I'd had to skip dinner, I knew something was different. No one had ever done that before! The crowd was humming with

11

anticipation. Then the lights dimmed, and the next three hours went by so fast I couldn't believe it was after 8:00!

I felt ready to burst if I didn't talk to someone about what I'd just seen, but I didn't know any real *LOTR* fans in my area. So I went home and finished my holiday newsletter, but instead of the usual stories of dog antics and travels, I raved about *The Fellowship of the Ring*. I'm sure my family and friends wondered if I'd lost it. But Julie, one of my friends back in Utah, read it and recognized a kindred spirit, so instead of just the annual note in the Christmas card, we started exchanging e-mails about *LOTR*. Both of us went back to the theater to see *FOTR* multiple times. When gardening season came, we took a break from the *LOTR* correspondence. Then *Pirates of the Caribbean* came out, and the e-mails flared up again, this time talking about our mutual admiration for Orlando Bloom/Legolas/Will Turner. I became a *TORn* regular, and discovered *The Council of Elrond* as well. There seemed no end to the Middle-earth riches on the internet.

When I was young and watched the first *Star Trek* series, I wished with all my child's heart that the universe of the Starship Enterprise and her crew was real. That I could somehow be a part of it. Now I felt the same way about Middle-earth — if only it was real, and I could just somehow get there. I suggested someone like Bill Gates should build a replica of Middle-earth in New Zealand, sort of a never-ending Renaissance fair. Not cheesy like some theme park, but with real buildings and citizens. You know Weta could do it. Sojourn with the Elves for a soul-soothing retreat; for a more rustic holiday, spend time with the hobbits of the Shire, or ride horses with the Rohirrim, another dream. *Middle-earth: The Resort* would make a fortune! I don't think most people realized I was only half-joking.

Julie and I bought the *FOTR* DVD as soon as it came out, and I discovered one of my co-workers, Carolyn, was also a *LOTR* fan. So now I had someone to talk to about *LOTR* face to face! By now my husband was beginning to think I was going a bit overboard with this *LOTR* thing. A few months after the *FOTR* DVD came out, I went to *The Two Towers* premiere. I got there quite early, and an informal line party formed. All of us Ringers began to talk about our favorite parts of *FOTR*, and what we expected to see in the next film. I began to wonder what it was about these films that drew so many people into animated conversations with complete strangers. That thought would stay in my mind throughout the next year, one where I probably spent too much time online talking to friends about *LOTR*.

Lest you think from all my enthusiasm for the *LOTR* films that they had replaced the book in my affections, you'd be dead wrong. The films re-kindled my interest in everything related to Middle-earth. I read *The Hobbit* and *The Lord of the Rings* at least once a year, but now I also listen to the wonderful Recorded Books version done by Rob Inglis even more often than that. It's the next best thing to reading it aloud.

I was one of those people who had never been able to get past the beginning of *The Silmarillion*. Then I listened to the recorded version done by Martin Shaw, and since then I have gone back to the book several times. I'm even beginning to be able to sort out all those names starting with F! Even though I already owned *The Silmarillion*, I bought the latest edition so I could have Ted Nasmith autograph it for me. Now when I re-read *The Lord of the Rings*, I understand all of Tolkien's references to the First and Second Ages, and it gives *LOTR* even more depth and poignancy.

There are still a good number of fans of the book who disapprove of the *LOTR* films, and it makes me very sad. For one thing, they represent two entirely different art forms, and should be judged as such. Although some of the authors in this book came to *The Lord of the Rings* via the films, almost every one of them has devoured all of Tolkien's written work as well.

In my job as a librarian, I saw the effect of the release of the films first-hand. People of all ages were clamoring for *LOTR* and anything else Tolkien had written. I still have trouble keeping enough copies of the books on the library shelves, even though the last film in the trilogy was released almost two years ago. It's my job to connect readers with books, and I especially love being able to give young readers the gift of *The Lord of the Rings*.

Lembas For the Soul

Something else wonderful took place the year that *The Two Towers* came out. I sat down and wrote my second piece of fan fiction, nearly 35 years after I wrote my first story about my beloved Elves. Then something unexpected happened. I'd published a romantic fantasy novel in the '90s, but had developed a severe case of writer's block after that. Writing my elven story tapped into the well of creativity I'd been trying to revive, and I started writing my own original fiction again, not fantasy this time, but a light, funny mystery. A part of my soul that had been frozen with fear suddenly took flight again.

The more time I spent with Ringers, either online or face-to-face, I realized that so many of us had been changed by our *LOTR* experience. I wanted to know more about this phenomenon, so the idea for a book of *LOTR* fans' true experiences took shape. Like the Professor, I ended up creating the sort of book I wanted to read. About the same time I decided to go ahead with the idea for *Lembas for the Soul*, I heard about the *Ringers: Lord of the Fans* film. I was excited about that project, too, and was disappointed I didn't get to a theater screening. But I thought there were more than enough Ringer stories to be told, especially since very few of us had the opportunity to participate in the film.

This past spring I set up my website, www.whitetreepress.com, to ask fans to send in their true *LOTR* experiences. I received many touching and heartfelt replies, too many to fit into one volume. It's been an honor and a pleasure to read them all, and then to share them with the *LOTR* community. I hope you will enjoy reading them as much as I have.

Catherine Kohman

Middle-earthlings

Karen Frisch

After we saw *The Fellowship of the Ring*, my husband and I shared so many inspired conversations about its heroes and villains that our daughter, Elizabeth, who was seven, couldn't resist joining in.

"Who's Aragorn?" she asked in suspense. "Who's Gollum?"

Allowing her to watch Merry and Pippin make mischief at Bilbo's birthday party couldn't do much harm, we thought. And if Elizabeth could see it, three-year-old Jennifer would want to, as well. We knew when we introduced our halflings to Tolkien's that we wanted them to grow up recognizing the characteristics of heroes and heroines. What better examples than those forged on the screen by Peter Jackson? The trilogy was a work of art to be handed down to future generations, we felt — especially ours.

The girls became so fascinated with *The Lord of the Rings* that they would ask us to tell them the stories while riding in the car. It's not easy to recite the plot of a three-and-a-half-hour movie while driving. My husband and I would pass the story off to each other when one tired or — heaven forbid — forgot what came next. Tolkien became bedtime reading and even bathtime reading. Elizabeth came to know the story so well she would correct us when we slipped up.

"Merry and Pippin are kidnapped by Uruk-hai, not orcs," she'd say. "They're a mix of orcs and goblin men that Saruman created, remember?"

As we watched our heavenly creatures turn into Middle-earthlings, we recognized personality traits from Tolkien's characters emerging. It was a relief when Jennifer's Gollum stage passed. We realized she was actually a hobbit, while her sister was an Elf. Our hobbit child, Jennifer, was young and round, her feet heavy when she ran and her sense of humor hearty, while Elizabeth, the Elf child, had grown reed-tall with long, straight

15

hair and a unique wisdom. The Fellowship was well represented in our family, with my husband one of the race of men and me undoubtedly a Dwarf (minus the beard).

Tolkien's characters became part of Elizabeth's study curriculum. She would ask us to invent *LOTR* math problems. "If Aragorn, Legolas, and Gimli are attacked by 12 orcs, and the orcs are joined by seven Uruk-hai and four Black Riders, how many enemies are they fighting?" we would ask.

Our Middle-earthlings developed new games related to *Lord of the Rings*. Our hobbit child was easy to pick up and run with while we shouted, "Give me the halfling!" We competed for the honor of playing an orc. "Looks like meat's back on the menu!" my husband would shout, nibbling on our hobbit child's leg.

"She is not for eating!" her sister and I would respond.

LOTR even made it to the checkerboard. After the first few checkers had been claimed, the remaining markers were assigned names. "I have Legolas," Elizabeth would say, "and here are Gandalf, Gimli, and — what's the name of Eowyn's brother?" No one was surprised when Aragorn and Gandalf were last on the board.

When we played *Oregon Trail,* a computer game that lets players travel back in time and face hazards encountered by the pioneers, we raised the stakes by renaming the computer-generated characters. We left room in our wagon for Legolas and Aragorn. Their presence didn't keep anyone from getting bitten by rattlesnakes, developing cholera, or dying of frostbite, but they made the game more exciting.

Our Middle-earthlings were thrilled when their dad brought home Nerf bows and arrows, for now they could practice their aim. While their skill fell short of Legolas's, it was fortunate the arrows were soft, since they could still inflict damage in the excitement of pretending.

My birthday gifts during that stretch included *LOTR* posters, the gorgeous elven brooch, and a book of Viggo's poetry. Elizabeth apologized for being able to find only 27 candles instead of the 48 to match my age, but I told her it didn't matter, since I had a long way to go until I reached "eleventy-one".

Tolkien's influence extended to pets as well. When the shelter mice we adopted turned out not to be two males as we'd been told, we had to find names for our new litter. Luckily, there were nine, and The Fellowship provided the names we needed.

While *The Lord of the Rings* fever has died down somewhat, the story made a permanent impression on our children. The characters have taken hold in their imaginations. Elf child Elizabeth's pen pal in her second-grade class is an Indian boy named Rohan.

"The Riders of Rohan!" she exclaimed. "I wonder if he knows about Eowyn and Eomer?"

Whether he does or not, she no longer has to ask the name of Eowyn's brother. I'm glad Peter Jackson's introduction to Tolkien has given her heroes who are more substantial than television's two-dimensional versions. And while meat isn't often on our menu, once the line entered our vocabulary, it never left.

The profound effect of the films on the young is a testament to their timelessness. Our Elf and hobbit children took their first step into the culture alongside Peter Jackson's characters. He captured Elf wisdom, Dwarf courage, human commitment and hobbit vulnerability poignantly and painstakingly, bringing justice to J.R.R. Tolkien's brilliance.

With Frodo and Sam introducing new generations of readers to Tolkien, our girls are in good company.

Biography: Karen Frisch. Karen lives in Rhode Island with her husband, two daughters adopted from China, and their dog, rabbit, mice, and fish. Author of *Unlocking the Secrets in Old Photographs* and *Creating Junior Genealogists: Tips and Activities for Family History Fun*, both published by Ancestry, she holds a Master's degree in English literature and a Bachelor's degree in art. She wishes that rather than waiting for *The Lord of the Rings* movies to come out she had discovered Tolkien years before she did.

Lembas for the Soul

Connections
Pam Bardwell

I first read *The Hobbit* and *The Lord of the Rings* trilogy when I was 13, which was more years ago than I care to say. At that time in history, peace, love, and protest were the norm. While I wasn't quite old enough to attend Woodstock — according to my mother — or march against the war, I still felt I was a child of the times ... part of a generation in search of answers. Many found those answers in Tolkien's books. They embraced his works and accepted them as part of their culture. To find those same answers, I, too, read the books. They took hold of me at once, but I had no one with whom to share them, since none of my friends at the time had read them. So I kept them to myself.

In the late 1970's, I was excited to learn a TV movie was being made of *The Hobbit*, a Rankin/Bass animated feature with Orson Bean as the voice of Bilbo. I remember settling in to watch the film and my disappointment with the end result. As a true fan, was this all that I had to look forward to? This now classic version of the telling of the tale was, shall we say, less than impressive. For the next three decades, whenever I thought of *The Hobbit*, I couldn't stop Orson Bean's voice from echoing in my mind.

Ralph Bakshi's animated version of *The Lord of the Rings* in 1978 did not impress me either, but rather made me realize that those of us who loved the books would have to settle for small screen animated films. If that was all we could hope for, that would have to do. Then I heard talk of a new *LOTR* live action film being produced. I caught the first glimpse of a teaser trailer – the Fellowship in single file, mounting a rise on the path from Rivendell. Could this truly be what I had been waiting for most of my life?

I wasn't ready to accept that reality — after all, I still had Orson Bean bouncing around in my brain. But true it was, and as the day approached for *The Fellowship of the Ring* to make its debut, I hesitated a bit. Waiting for the reviews, I didn't make plans to see it until a few weeks after it opened, just in case it was going to be another disappointment. I am at a point in my life where my tastes are more discerning and I wasn't ready to just accept another Rankin/Bass attempt at creating entertainment from those beloved books.

On January 5th, 2002 — my birthday — my husband and I entered the theater, he there by default, since it was my turn to pick the movie. He had never read the books or seen any of the early films, and quite frankly didn't want to be there. As the theater darkened and Howard Shore's music began, I knew at that moment my world was about to change forever. I could feel joy welling up inside of me. *This was it*, what I had waited nearly 35 years for! It was about to begin, and this time I would have someone to share it with. The three hours flew by. I was left at the end of Part One craving more — it would be torture to have to wait another year to experience Part Two. I sat through the credits just to make sure Orson Bean was not listed anywhere. He was not.

As we left the theater that afternoon, I told my husband I would be going back to see the film again the following weekend. He politely declined to accompany me. He said it was too long and too confusing. Having never read the books, he found it difficult to follow and far too many characters to keep up with. Thoughts of having made a convert of him faded quickly and I resigned myself to sharing this experience with the strangers who surrounded me in the theater at each showing.

Yet even as strangers we made a connection, since I would see some of the same faces each time I went. We smiled at one another and nodded in agreement that there was nowhere else we would rather be at that moment. I managed three more trips back to the theater during *The Fellowship's* run, and then found myself in giddy (a word that has never been used to describe me by anyone who knows me) anticipation of the DVD to be released in August of 2002. The day it went on sale, I purchased my copy and watched it twice in one evening. I also spent time prior to the release of *The Two Towers* re-reading the books so I could prepare myself for the films yet to come.

During this time, without my knowledge, my husband had purchased *The Lord of the Rings* audio books on CD and was secretly listening to them in his car to and from work each day. When I finally discovered what he was up to, he remarked that since *The Lord of the Rings* had become such an important part of my life, he wanted to share it. In order to do that, he felt he needed to understand it better. What a welcome surprise for me — I had a convert after all!

I have since gone on to see *The Two Towers* 12 times in the theaters and *The Return of the King* 15 times before it ended its theatrical run. While my husband accompanied me at least once to each film, my convert says there are limits to his interest, so he didn't go with me to every show. I understand he will never be called a "Ringer", but I take pride in knowing I have turned him from the Dark Side — oh, wait, wrong trilogy — *enlightened* him on all things Tolkien.

In addition to sharing my *Lord of the Rings* experiences with my husband, I've also had some impact on others around me as well. One former coworker and I have formed a bond through our love for the books and films. She has dubbed me Mrs. V (Viggo) since I had actually heard of him and admired his film work prior to *The Fellowship* and she had not. Another former coworker and I held our own home version of Trilogy Tuesday — we sat together and watched *The Fellowship of the Ring* Extended Edition, then *The Two Towers* EE immediately following, then headed for the movie theater that night to experience *The Return of the King* together. Great fun!

In conversations with my 83-year-old mother, she remembered back to the '60s when I had read all of the books, but she found it hard to understand how I could sit through the same film so many times. Still, knowing how much the films meant to me, she actually stayed up well past her bedtime and watched the entire Academy Awards ceremony in 2004 just to see "my movie", as she calls it, make a clean sweep and take all 11 awards.

Lembas for the Soul

I wear a ring I purchased on the internet last year, a silver spinning ring with writing engraved around it. When I recently visited my doctor, she asked what words were written on my ring because it looked *elvish*! When I confirmed it was, we chatted about her love for the books, how she had read them so many years ago, and her thoughts on the movies as well. Another connection made.

It's human nature to seek out and connect with others who share common interests, to feel a sense of belonging. It gives us our sense of self and strengthens us in our daily pursuits. It has been a journey of discovery for me: first to connect with the books all those years ago, then the long wait for the right technology and the right person to come along who could translate such beloved books to the screen so well. Still more importantly, I value my connections with others around me and the opportunity to share *The Lord of the Rings* experience. I have lost count of the number of times I have watched the DVDs at home — both theatrical version and extended editions — of all three films. They are, in my opinion, magnificent works of art and thanks to Peter Jackson, his cast and crew, Orson Bean's voice is finally out of my head.

Biography: Pam Bardwell. "Born and raised in upstate New York, I currently live and work near Rochester. I lived for several years in Las Vegas, NV, but missed the greens of spring and the autumn colors of my home state. I have been married to my husband, Dave, for 22 years. We have four cats that allow us to live with them: Annie, Gracie, Christy, and Dorsey."

Lembas For the Soul

One Ring to Bind Them
Colleen Joan Duffy

When you first open *The Fellowship of the Ring* and read the lines about the Rings of Power, you absolutely know the story you're about to read is going to be something special!

I'm a new Ringer. I confess I hadn't read the book when the films came out, but now I'm totally enthralled. It's as if I've made this amazing discovery. After seeing (and being completely absorbed by) the first two films, I then read the book. I still remember the exact moment when I finished it — New Year's Day, 2004, on the beach with my family. I hated having to say goodbye to Frodo at the Grey Havens. Since then, I often delve into the book. I keep thinking of things I want to look up, and then I get lost in Middle-earth and am late for work.

A film often doesn't live up to the book, but for me, every aspect of the *LOTR* films is brilliantly done. The actors fit their characters so well; the costumes, weapons, sets, landscapes, creatures, special effects, languages, script — there's nothing that makes you think, "No, that's not right!". From a purely female point of view, Viggo Mortensen is simply breathtaking as Aragorn. I must also mention Howard Shore's music. Each piece seems to fit perfectly in the scene and the songs are hauntingly beautiful, expertly performed by all those different and stunning voices.

I've watched the films so often, yet every time I become totally immersed in Middle-earth from those opening minutes of Galadriel's prologue to the very end of the credits in ROTK. I play certain scenes more than once and I always watch the trilogy as a whole. There's no way that I can just watch one and leave it at that.

My family thinks I'm nuts to be so enthusiastic because they don't like fantasy. I keep telling them it's so much more than that! It's not just about weird and wonderful creatures or big battles and big special effects. There's friendship, loyalty, love, humour, courage, hope, despair, betrayal, tragedy and especially, perseverance against all odds. Big scenes that take your breath away, but also quiet moments which draw you into the lives of the characters.

Often, during a conversation about a subject which is totally unrelated to *LOTR*, a word or a phrase will immediately send me to Middle-earth and I'll say, "That reminds me of a scene in *LOTR*!" and go on to describe it. People just roll their eyes at me and say, "Not again!"

I have no creative talents myself, but I truly appreciate not only the story, but also the poetry in Tolkien's book; e.g. the poem written by Frodo for Gandalf, the poem of The Ents, *The Song of the Great Eagle* and *The Riddle of Strider*. And then you have the beautiful Elvish languages, with words like *mae govannen* (well met), *namárië* (farewell), *mellon nîn* (my friend).

I've also discovered Viggo is a poet, and reading some of his work has opened my mind to new ways of thinking. In fact, writing this story is my first attempt to be a bit creative — trying to find the right words to express my thoughts and feelings.

In October this year I'll be visiting Middle-earth to see those stunning landscapes for myself. I'll be doing things I've never done before: riding in helicopters, hot air balloons, jet boats and river rafting. I'll be meeting new people (other Ringers!), so *LOTR* is bringing people together and adding immeasurably to my life. I've learned some Maori words in preparation for my trip, so that's another new experience for me because of *LOTR*.

Reading the book, as well as watching the films, has been, and continues to be, an emotional adventure. It's brought me so much unexpected enjoyment, like finding a web site where they tell you your hobbit and elven names: I'm Orangeblossom Millstone of Bywater and Celebriän Vanimeldë!

The Lord of the Rings has also made me appreciate life more, and I now live with a more positive attitude. I enjoy cycling and I was trying to get up quite a steep hill. I felt I wasn't going to make it, and then I found myself thinking of Sam and Frodo and the way they kept going, even though they'd been through so much and were totally exhausted. I thought, "Well, if they could keep going, then I can surely get up this hill!" And I did!

Namárië!!

Biography: Colleen Joan Duffy. "I was born in 1963 and live in Grahamstown, South Africa. I am single and have one brother and one sister. I work as a secretary in an accounting firm. I have a multitude of interests: *The Lord of the Rings* (surprise!!), movies of almost any kind, reading fiction, Elvis Presley, music (C&W, easy listening, soul), travelling, animals (especially cats), nature (e.g. the sea), casual walking and cycling, coffee, chocolate, talking and family (this is not deliberately last on my list...just the order in which things happened to pop into my mind!)."

Born to the Rings
Anna Ochitkov

When I brought my second baby home from the hospital, I knew *The Lord of the Rings* would forever be associated with the births of both my sons.

Being a big fan of the book, I was extremely excited to see the story on the big screen. I was two months pregnant when *The Fellowship of the Ring* came out in theatres. It quickly became one of my favorite movies. The visual images stayed in my mind through my entire pregnancy. Whenever I sang to my unborn baby or tried to relax, I would picture myself in The Shire.

When it came time for labor, I brought a printout of The Shire to the hospital as a focal point to help me concentrate. I didn't look at it once. During the most intense contractions, I kept picturing Galadriel kissing my forehead. Now let me explain: I was not a fanatic, so the whole visions-of-Elves thing was a big shock to me. In fact, I was pretty embarrassed even telling my husband about it.

Leo was born on August 5, 2002, the day before *The Fellowship of the Ring* came out on DVD. My husband, being the funny guy that he is, brought the DVD to the hospital. He said it was the most appropriate present he could give me then. So we watched the movie on his laptop, right there in the maternity ward of the hospital. The first music my son heard was the soundtrack from *The Fellowship of the Ring*.

I had never read *The Hobbit*, so I decided to read it during my maternity leave. Since the baby was always with me, I read the book out loud to him to get him familiar with my voice. This meant that the first book I read to him would be *The Hobbit*. By this time, I was beginning to think I might be a fanatic after all.

Since then, I have read all the Tolkien books. I recorded every television special on the subject of *The Lord of the Rings*. I even dragged my poor husband to a sci-fi convention and Renaissance fair. Next up is an elvish tattoo. At this point, my friends are beginning to think I'm certifiable.

After *The Return of the King* Extended Edition came out on DVD, I decided to re-read the books. A week later, I learned I was pregnant. I don't know whatever elven magic was at work here, but it was a perfect theme for my pregnancy (again). Because I now had a two-year-old, it took me the entire pregnancy to read the books. When I was nine months pregnant, there was a special screening of the *LOTR* Trilogy at the IMAX theatres in Toronto. It was an amazing experience, except no pregnant woman should be allowed to sit for that long. By the end of the movie, I had hobbit's feet.

When it was time to have this baby, I was swimming in *The Lord of the Rings*. There were no visions or posters on the wall this time. There was no time. The baby came so fast, my epidural didn't start working until *after* the baby was born. I experienced déjà vu when my husband produced a familiar DVD and a laptop. We watched *The Fellowship* for about two minutes before we fell asleep. The nurse had to wake us up to turn off the movie, because the girl lying next to us said the Moria orcs kept her up. Thank God she was a fan!

The next day, my husband gave me the most amazing gift. It was the One Ring in a beautiful wooden presentation box. I recognized it instantly. It was the official Ring from the movie. I had been on the internet for the past year drooling over that ring. It has now replaced my wedding ring.

Now that we're home again, I'm re-reading *The Hobbit*. Out loud.

My friends are planning an intervention. We named our second baby Sam.

Lembas for the Soul

A Hobbit-sized biography: Anna Ochitkov. "Alex and I met when I was 15 and Alex was 17. The same year, we read *The Lord of the Rings* together for the first time. Coincidence? I think not.

This story is for Leo and Sam. I hope you will be entertained to see what frame of mind your parents were in when we had you."

In My Daughter's Eyes
Christopher Fenoglio

Strolling into the auditorium after the bell, my daughter's friends and classmates slowly took their seats. Getting out of regular class for a video presentation was a rare event and they were going to savor every minute.

"Your dad is going to talk about *The Lord of the Rings* films?" they asked Kristin. "Yes," she told them, silently praying that I would not embarrass her in front of her friends.

I was saying the same prayer myself.

The school's Theology Department had invited me to speak on the religious themes in the three Peter Jackson films. But with just a PowerPoint presentation and a videotape, could I keep her friends entertained for the next 90 minutes? What if they were not fans of *The Lord of the Rings* like me? Would I waste their time, or would they be inspired? Most importantly, what will my daughter think after her father speaks to the entire junior class of her high school?

I got the invitation because months ago, I wrote three articles for our local diocesan newspaper. Writing about religious themes in popular culture, especially films, is one of my passions.

The editors liked my short devotionals about the three main characters: Frodo, who time and time again made a conscious, willful decision to do everything he could to fulfill the quest; Gollum, who struggled with the good and bad within himself and who found a trusting response from Frodo, but a suspicious one from Sam; and Aragorn, who conquered his own doubts and became all that he could be to defeat Sauron the Deceiver.

I could center my speech on these themes, but I was still not sure I could keep the attention of the students. High school students can get bored so quickly. They would probably want more.

Perhaps they would be interested to hear how I flew to Hollywood for the press viewing of the third and final film, *The Return of the King*. I could describe how I checked into the luxurious Four Seasons Hotel in Beverly Hills and later met Sir Ian McKellen (Gandalf) and producer Barry Osborne that evening in the lounge.

I could also tell the students how we had to surrender our cell phones and cameras before we were admitted into the theater. New Line Cinema wanted to prevent images from being uploaded onto the internet two weeks before the film was released. I could describe how we sat there with an Arwen bag of popcorn and an Aragorn cup of Diet Coke, cheering for Eowyn when she slew the Witch-King of Angmar and tearing during Sam's determined words to Frodo — "I can carry you."

No, these stories might hold their attention for a little while longer, but it wouldn't last. The students needed more details to help them relate to the films on a deeper, more personal level.

After showing excerpts from the three films and summarizing the main religious themes, I asked the students "If you could have a real conversation with one of the actors, what would you say to him or her?"

Without waiting for an answer, I described the interviews that I conducted on the morning after previewing *The Return of the King*. In a small room with 12 other religious journalists, we sat around a small table with an empty chair. One by one, for 20 minutes at a time, the actors, writers, producers, composer and director sat with us and discussed the film.

Not only did we learn lots of background details on script composition and the filmmaking process, we also saw the actors in a brand new light. Each of them had developed a strong connection with the character they portrayed. Many of the actors also shared personal insights to their work, insights that left a lasting impression on me.

For instance:

♦ Elijah Wood (Frodo) — a thoughtful and energetic young man who said his scenes with Smeagol/Gollum were motivated by a caring nature for someone addicted to a powerful substance.

♦ Dominic Monaghan (Merry) and Billy Boyd (Pippin) — two pals who not only had a good time, but also took up the cause of caring for the environment, especially worldwide reforestation projects.

♦ Andy Serkis (Smeagol/Gollum) — a humble man who was genuinely thankful when we praised his work.

♦ Sean Astin (Sam) — an accomplished actor who said the best part of the filming process was that his family could be with him in New Zealand.

♦ Liv Tyler (Arwen) — a newlywed who implored our students to "be nice to each other" and "care for your friends."

♦ Orlando Bloom (Legolas) — who in a quiet but well-spoken manner, talked about Elves and Dwarves getting along as friends. If they can get along, why can't other people follow their example?

As I described these real people and the motivations behind their acting, the students listened and watched with great attention.

I hoped that they would identify with the actors, realizing that they share many of the same feelings, insecurities, desires for stable relationships and the need to be part of a cause for the greater good. By taking care of their friends, preserving the environment and respecting the cultures of people they don't know, these high school students could help make our own world a better place in which to live. For as Galadriel says to Frodo in the first film, "Even the smallest person can change the course of the future."

As I finished my speech and the lunch bell rang, the students rose to leave the auditorium. My daughter and a few of her friends, however, walked down the aisle towards me.

"Dad," she said, "that was pretty cool."

I smiled and said "thanks," knowing that those words were indeed high praise from my teenage daughter.

Biography: Christopher Fenoglio. Thirty years ago Christopher Fenoglio was given the paperback editions of *The Lord of the Rings* and has been a fan of the books and films ever since. As a reporter and freelance writer he has interviewed numerous actors, authors and sports figures. Fenoglio's column "Reel Life," syndicated to Catholic newspapers, relates Christian themes in popular films to life experiences in today's culture. He is currently writing a children's book about Santa Claus and his own screenplay adaptation of *The Hobbit*. He lives in Nashville with his wife and three teenagers. He can be reached at chrisfenoglio@alumni.nd.edu.

Touched by Fire
Anne Londez

The Lord of the Rings actually changed my life in a very concrete, although quite roundabout, way. I have been a *LOTR* fan for almost 20 years, from my first reading of the book. However, when *The Fellowship of the Ring* came out, I thought I would be disappointed with the adaptation, as I always had been with books I loved. So at first, I refused to see it.

When *The Two Towers* was released, I was still in the same frame of mind. But when at last *The Return of the King* came out, I grew curious. Since the first two were available in DVD, I decided to rent them and give them a chance ... and I loved them so much that I instantly bought the extended editions and watched them over and over again, for months. I also got onto the *theOneRing.net* (*TORn*) forums and met many other fans. Since I am French and live in Switzerland, it meant I would eventually travel to the United States, but there is more to the story than that.

I suppose the reason why those films affected me so much is because there was a truth in everything the cast and crew were doing, an intrinsic integrity that I have rarely encountered before. I was amazed to see Tolkien's world come to life in such a realistic way, and naturally I wanted to know more about the people who had made that possible. I avidly watched and read everything I could find about the cast and crew.

Viggo Mortensen was the first one to really touch me, first for his acting, and then for his real-life personality. At that time, I was drastically re-organizing my life to accommodate my deep personal need for *integrity*, and I was struck by the fact that everybody who talked about Viggo used that precise word. I read everything I could find about him and realized he had achieved the sort of life I would like to have. Not the fame and money part, of course, but his ability to live by his art and convictions with as little compromise as possible. I also appreciated the fact that his art was not limited to one specific medium. I've always needed to do different things at the same time, or I get bored. When I read about him and he said the exact same thing (and lots of other things I could have said, too), it was almost spooky. When he was interviewed about why he did so many different things, his answer was, 'A creator creates.' Viggo's words have stayed in my mind since that moment.

A few months before this happened, I had decided to quit my job as a scientist to go full time into glass-making. I wanted to do this mostly for ethical reasons, but also because I needed more creative space. I had thought of keeping a foot in the corporate world by teaching certain subjects in which I had experience, like presentation techniques, but living the *LOTR* adventure and knowing someone like Viggo existed made me realize I shouldn't compromise. I really didn't want to have anything to do with the corporate world anymore, and I wanted to explore pure creativity full time. The amount of unbridled creativity I sensed while watching the documentaries about the making of the films was in itself very inspiring, making me long to have been a part of it.

While learning more about who Viggo was, I realized I loved everything he was doing: writing, painting, music, and photography. I began to think that since I felt so keenly close to him in spirit, there was no reason why I shouldn't try to do the same. I had been involved in music since childhood, and had tried photography in my teens. I bought brushes and canvas and started painting, with no previous training, although I had a solid art education in my youth. I also started writing poetry, first in a style inspired by Tolkien, as I was re-reading the books at that time.

Both experiences were exhilarating, as if for the first time in my life I was able to let flow things I didn't know I had in me.

33

I sold my first big painting a few months ago (although that was not my aim in the first place) which included parts of a poem I wrote that was definitely inspired by Viggo. People who see my work often think I am a classically trained painter, which is both weird and gratifying, since I never took any sort of class. But I think what the *LOTR* experience (and Viggo's example) made me realize is that if you are honestly expressing who you are without compromising, the result touches people. It comforted me in the thought that I had taken the right path and should not doubt who I really was.

What's more, people around me sensed the change in me and I've had really amazing experiences sharing my newly found freedom. I think it has made me more open towards others, and also more sharing and less critical. It improved my teaching, too. Even some of my long-standing glass students said things to me that they'd never said before, about how coming to my studio provided them with a free space that was very important in their life. I was very touched. All that from a novel and movie ...

Peter Jackson must be a really amazing person to have been able not only to bring Tolkien's world to life so perfectly, but also to catalyze such things; in putting together the movie he was able to push people to go beyond themselves in a constant search for the true spirit of Tolkien. In doing that to such an extent he necessarily influenced viewers to do the same. I am indebted to him and his team for helping me push my life-changing experience a whole step further, creatively speaking.

Biography: Anne Londez. A scientist by education, Anne Londez realized at the ripe age of 34 that the art world had far more to offer than her professional job. She resolutely turned her back on the corporate world as she plunged into the world of glass art. Educated in flamework both in the US and Murano, Italy, she now spends her days staring at molten glass and trying to share her passion by teaching the wonderful art of glass bead-making in Switzerland. Visit her website at: annedesigns.netfirms.com.

In the Fellowship's Footsteps
Shirley McCarter

"Why does Shirley love *The Lord of the Rings* movies so much?"

This question is one that has been repeated among my dearest friends, who were not so enamored by the films as I was. This question is one that even I had to ask, after a bit of time, as my love of the films increased, instead of waning like it had for many other films.

FRIENDSHIP
Unwavering
Protective
Faithful
True

COURAGE   **HONOR**
LOYALTY
New friends are like silver
Old friends are like gold
Definitely both are a valuable treasure

These movies first captured my heart because of the relationships I saw forming in *The Fellowship of the Ring*. The relationships that first attracted me then grew through so many trials that I became fully involved in the stories. Throughout the following two films — *The Two Towers* and *The Return of the King* — I was hooked! I found myself identifying with various characters in the stories as my own life unfolded.

Sometimes I felt like Frodo ... a little person facing a seemingly impossible task. But with the aid of his true and noble friends, he could find strength for the battles he must endure.

35

Sometimes I felt like Sam ... the faithful sidekick who must remain steady and true in order to help a friend when the struggles threaten to overcome even the stoutest heart.

Merry and Pippin are special to me for their playful innocence and willingness to face unknown danger to help out their dear friend.

I admire the other members of The Fellowship: Gandalf, Aragorn, Legolas, Gimli and Boromir, who are all willing to battle overwhelming dark forces to help the Ring Bearer complete his mission.

The Return of the King had me weeping at so many different scenes. The coronation of Aragorn made me yearn for the day when my own King will return to claim his bride. The separation of the hobbits at various points in the movie had me crying, since these scenes reminded me of the worst part of military life: saying goodbye to those who have become so dear, uncertain if we will ever see one another again on this Earth. I was sobbing uncontrollably by the end of my first viewing of this film, because I knew I would have to deal with this *again* soon. At that time, I could not deal with one more set of best friends being separated, neither in our real world, nor Tolkien's fantasy world.

As I continued to wrestle with the way these movies had taken over my thought life, my prayer became, "Why can I not get this out of my head? Am I being obsessive? Are you trying to teach me something? Please open my eyes!"

The Tolkien-created characters that became so dear to me exemplified a verse that reads, "Greater love has no one than this, that one lay down his life for his friends." Being casual friends is one thing, but have we lost that sacrificial love for others? To possess that kind of a love for another is such a rare gift.

As I pondered the friendships in the movie, a question surfaced: "Am I that kind of friend? Have I ever had a friend such as this?" The first question, I cannot answer. As for the second, a dear high school classmate instantly came to mind. I can still see Corey's smiling face to this day. A young man who would have been willing to step between us and a gun that had been pointed at us. A young man with courage and a love for others that went beyond self-preservation. I hope wherever he is today that he has been blessed for such bravery.

When the *LOTR* films came out, my family and I were living in North Dakota. The environment was harsh, but the people were nice. We discovered many treasured friends in Grand Forks, but there was one particular group with whom the bond went much deeper. Through the trials of marriage difficulties, lost babies, illnesses, husbands deployed, childhood traumas resurfacing and much counseling, to the joys of babies born, marriages restored, hopes renewed and a true-to-life miracle, our families were fused together with a bond of friendship that is stronger than any I had previously experienced in my lifetime. To me, The Fellowship of the movies became reality in the true-life fellowship we were experiencing. I will be forever grateful for the blessing of these friendships forged by the fires of life.

It was encouraging to read and see how the *LOTR* cast and crew also bonded through the filming of these movies. No one enjoys trials and hardships, but if we keep our eyes and our hearts open, we may just find that all the pressure has turned some of our lumps of coal into treasured and valuable diamonds.

Biography: Shirley McCarter. Mrs. Shirley McCarter was born and spent much of her childhood in Charleston, West Virginia. After moving to Omaha, Nebraska, in her teens, she met and married her high school sweetheart. They have been blessed with three boys, a faithful canine companion, and a host of friends whose life stories, love and encouragement enriches their life journey. They are currently living in England. Her favorite verse is "You will seek me and find me when you seek me with all your heart." Jeremiah 29:13.

Passing the Torch
Matthew Jacobsmeyer

Fall 2003

The other night, I furiously logged on to the web, just bursting to hear the new song from the ROTK soundtrack by Annie Lennox. And when I heard it, it truly moved me, but in a completely unexpected way. The reason: it reminded me of something that I knew deep down, but had nearly forgotten.

It's almost over.

I've waited two years — no, *five* years — for this moment. For this movie. For this epic to be complete. Logging on to this website, going to *Lordoftherings.net* every day, rereading the books, reading articles, seeing reports, discussing it with friends ...everything. It has been on my mind constantly, the anticipation building for half a decade. Each movie (and DVD) teasing with more info, hinting at more to come. And now, we are in the final stretch.

And it ... is almost ... over.

No more anticipating. No more waiting. No more "Will they do this?" or "Will we see that?" It will be done. It will be ***over***.

Hearing that song made me realize that when I see credits rolling with it, there will be no more movies left. And it reminded me of my dad, and what he told me about the first time he read The Books.

He was about 14 or 15. He played some football, held down a job and studied quite a bit. He had no spare time to himself, but one day, my grandmother gave him three paperback books she had just read. "I think you'll like these," she told him, "but make sure you get through the first 50 pages or so; it's a little slow in the beginning." While working all weekend, while going to school, while playing football and practicing, he read those books.

38

He read them like a madman. He gave up sleeping to read them, because he needed to see how the Fellowship escaped Moria, how Merry and Pippin would be saved from the orcs, how Frodo would be affected by Gollum and the One Ring. He read for four days straight, until he reached the end, needing to know how the story would finish, how the characters would end up. And when he got to the last page, he closed the book, and did something quite unexpected.

He started to cry.

A teenager, my father, alone, gently weeping with a book in his hands.

This stunned me the first time he told me this story. My father is not exactly an emotional creature, and the thought of him bawling over a book baffled me. I remember asking him, "Why did you cry?"

"Because I knew, from that moment on, that I could never read it again for the first time."

As I sat there listening to Annie Lennox, I understood that feeling. Yes, there will be an extended edition next year, and they have been so marvelous to date that there is no doubt it will exceed what we see in December, but it still won't be the first time. It won't move us as deeply as that initial moment, that surprise we will get when we actually see it on screen. Yes, we know the ending already; yes, we know what happens to all the characters, but it will only be truly unique once.

And then, it's over.

That's the problem with wanting something so much. It is as if we all have Gollum inside of us: we want the Ring, but what would we actually do with it once we have it? What will we feel on December 18th? As happy as I will be to see the movie, how sad will I feel that it is finally over? How will I feel once I see it for the first time, for the last time?

For the last two years, I have seen *LOTR* with my father on opening day, and we will be doing the same this year. It's my birthday gift to him — we see it for the first time, together. This year, after watching it, as I hear Annie Lennox in the background,

I will turn to my side. I will look into my father's eyes, and see what he thinks. And I will know how he feels, for I will feel it, too. And unlike before, he will not be alone.

Perhaps we'll cry together.

Biography: Matthew Jacobsmeyer. Matthew "Vilyakeeper" Jacobsmeyer lives in Rancho Cordova, California, and has been a Tolkien fan since he was a young teenager. He received the gift of *LOTR* from his father, who in turn had been given the book by his mother. As Matthew's friends can attest, he can talk about the book until he (or the listener) is blue in the face, a skill that amazes and terrifies them at the same time. Family reunions can lead to Tolkien-inspired conversations that would make *The Council of Elrond* look like a TV commercial.

And yes, he wears a ring set with a blue gemstone.

Eowyn and the Witch-King

Hearing the Horns of Rohan

Ever Onward–
Following Tolkien's Lead
Lynnette Porter

At the age of 14, I discovered and fell in love with *The Lord of the Rings.* This discovery was surprising in a couple of ways: 1) I hadn't particularly cared for *The Hobbit,* although its cover on the rack of paperbacks in the high school library intrigued me enough to read the book one weekend, and 2) as Bilbo warned, once I stepped out onto the *Rings* road, I was swept along to who knows where. I still don't know exactly where my *Rings*-related journey will end, only that it has been a glorious path.

If someone had told me that during the next 30-plus years Professor Tolkien would inspire me to travel around the world, write chapters or even a whole book, and teach classes related to *The Lord of the Rings,* that amazing prediction would have seemed as likely as Bilbo appearing in my living room to tell me all about Smaug and a certain wizard. I owe a great deal of inspiration for my work to J.R.R. Tolkien, and especially to the hobbits and Gandalf, and I must thank them for indirectly providing me with some of the best experiences in my life.

During my high school years, Tolkien competed with Steinbeck and Michener for my spare time, but throughout my 20's, 30's, and 40's, other later literary obsessions faded. I returned to the Shire often, and each time, I related to different characters.

I first identified with Éowyn. Sadly, my physical prowess would never match hers, but sometimes I felt left out, too. I understood all too clearly that women sometimes have to convince themselves and others that they are capable leaders with their own dreams to fulfill. With Éowyn, I shared a love of horses, and during my youth and early adulthood I rode as often as possible. How easy it was to pretend that we two young blonde women charged together toward our destinies!

As an older sibling, I frequently believed myself a "Merry" who shared adventures and misfortunes with a younger brother — or cousin, as the case may be. Like Merry, I loved and eventually wrote books. (In fact, Merry's treatises on pipeweed could even be construed as technical writing, the subject of my graduate degrees.) Perhaps I still am most like Merry, the planner who feels the need to look out for others.

Once I became a teacher, I thought of the many educators who served as my mentors and role models. Not surprisingly, Gandalf stepped forward as clearly as any of my human guides. Gandalf taught me by example what a teacher should be: humorous and kindly at times, but stern and demanding at others. Through whatever experience, Gandalf steadfastly supports his friends and charges. I hope to be that kind of teacher. My world is much richer because these citizens of Middle-earth are my neighbors.

By the time that Peter Jackson's film adaptation arrived, I was eager to visit the Shire again, but armed with insights into characters and their dilemmas gleaned through more than a quarter century's study. What more could I learn?

To my surprise, I learned a lot. Although the books and films differ in the particulars of plot or character, I love (but criticize) them both. I love the characters in print and enjoy their quiet moments on screen. I cringe in the extended DVD editions when Éowyn attempts to cook or Gimli challenges Legolas to a drinking game. However, I'm also frustrated that Tolkien didn't describe what happened when Gimli found Pippin under that troll, or how Merry and Pippin were reunited after Cormallen. (Thank goodness for film-inspired fan fiction to "fill up the corners" and sate my voracious appetite for detail.)

Jackson showed me not only the Shire, but more importantly, that it can exist today. Until I visited New Zealand, I doubted that the lush countryside shown on film could be real; my subsequent visit to Matamata convinced me. New Zealand revealed majesties that sometimes, for example, during a hike to a glacier in the Southern Alps, quite literally took my breath. If nothing else, I thank Peter Jackson for visually introducing me to New Zealand, which encouraged me to visit the country, first during a series of academic conferences, and later to visit friends and tour both islands.

Jackson's adaptation also convinced me that Tolkien's tale is still relevant today, even if it wins some new fans' interest only because of the on-screen battles or special effects. Those brought into the theatre to see spectacular feats of cinematic wizardry also might leave with an understanding of why family and friends are so important, and how loyalty and faith can change the course of the world.

The themes of friendship, love, hope, and courage resonate across the years. Especially in a new millennium, when life seems more perilous than ever, moviegoers need screen as well as literary heroes who do more than slash and burn, seek and destroy. Audiences need characters who fight for their families and friends, but realize the enormity of the costs of war, who want to bring people (or Elves, Dwarves, and hobbits) together in a peaceful world. *The Lord of the Rings* provides that ideal, and those in the future who attend anniversary screenings or share DVDs with their children and grandchildren may all be influenced by the Professor's world.

The revival of all things Tolkien in the early 2000's encouraged me to lend my voice to the discussion of these themes. I decided to write another book, this time about my favorite characters in *LOTR*. (I'd written four books earlier in my career, but nothing regarding literature or film.) Writing outside my comfort zone was scary, but the films inspired me to conduct more research about Tolkien and his works. I read hundreds of critical books and articles and watched as many hours of broadcasts or interviews regarding the adaptation. Film viewing became my late-evening routine, as did writing for hours on weekends. Thus, *Unsung Heroes of The Lord of the Rings: From the Page to the Screen* was born in 2005. For a while, *LOTR* was bad for my social life, but it eventually provided me with new friends worldwide who share a love of the story.

The wealth of information gathered during my research prompted me to develop a new university course for honors students. They analyze *The Lord of the Rings* as hero literature, but we also watch the films together. We cheer our favorite characters and thrill to the action sequences. More importantly, we discuss the themes emphasized in the films and book. My students often get carried away in their discussions, and they soon go off to learn more about Tolkien's other works, the places where the adaptation was filmed, and the myths that influenced the Professor as a writer. The road goes ever on . . . what Tolkien and other teachers/authors, such as Tom Shippey, taught me is now being passed on to another generation. I hope my students find *LOTR* memorable, at least, and at best, inspiring. Perhaps they also will guide someone toward Middle-earth.

As an academic, I often present papers about various aspects of my teaching or writing. Because of Tolkien and Jackson, I've traveled around the U.S. to discuss my favorite characters. I've visited and plan to return to New Zealand. My journeys led me to England, in part to visit the places where Tolkien lived and worked. However, I also shared with other fans and scholars a love of *The Lord of the Rings,* as the Tolkien Society commemorated the 50th anniversary of publication. Although I probably would have traveled outside the U.S. (I have the un-hobbit-like desire to leave home and see the world), I might not have gone as far as New Zealand or made internet friends in England. My travels and life have been enriched not only by literature and films, but also by the scholars, critics, and fans.

Little did I know when I checked out my first yellowed copy of *The Fellowship of the Ring* that my Middle-earth adventures would take me so far or let me meet so many people. We are all part of a miraculous web spun from one man's imagination, a web much friendlier than Shelob's, but one that has ensnared us nevertheless. When I see my students reading *The Lord of the*

Rings, or when I sit with other fans in a darkened auditorium to share the journey through Middle-earth, I only hope that their travels along the Tolkien trail are as varied and happy as mine have been.

Biography: Lynnette Porter. Lynnette geographically lives in Florida, but philosophically resides in Middle-earth. She teaches at Embry-Riddle Aeronautical University and writes non-fiction books, chapters and conference papers about film, literature, and television, as well as online education and technical communication. She is a devoted *LOTR* fan and can often be found at fantasy and science fiction conferences.

Lembas for the Soul

A Twist in the Story
Michelle Hillman

June 16th, 2003, was the first time that I can remember feeling my soul leap. This was the day I found *The Lord of the Rings* and, while not that long ago, it feels as if I have traveled with the Fellowship for a lifetime. Life has perpetually changed for the better since that rousing moment, when I finally realized one important thing: *this is what I have been searching for.*

Being raised in a small, rural town in western New York with twice as many cows as people, there was little room for adventure. As do most students, I struggled with developing an identity. I ached to be accepted among the elite population of the popular, and in doing so lost my true self. It was not until losing a childhood dream, and almost losing a child I watched grow up as a neighbor, that I realized how precious and fragile life truly is. When *The Lord of the Rings* entered my life, first with the movies and quickly followed by the books, I was just starting to grow up at the age of 17.

The Lord of the Rings caused me to grow younger, actually.

I say this not in a facetious manner, but with reverence and utmost respect. As it happened, this "fantasy" thing was one I had publicly scorned for many years. In my quest to become one of the chosen few who would obtain all their heart's desires by having popularity and numerous significant others, I thought fantasy just wasn't cool.

Upon further reflection, I must laugh heartily at myself for my blindness and naiveté.

The realm of fantasy is a beautiful thing. It is a world where tales of honor, glory and courage fuse together to become one

47

grand adventure. Races bond together with one common and noble goal, and we are drawn into permanent residence within the pages of a fantasy novel. In counterpoint to a modern world of gluttony, hate and dishonesty, fantasy offers a true emotional range of experiences, regardless of the fact that the characters and plot are fictional.

We finally learn to feel in fantasy.

When I was first introduced to this new world, I had mixed feelings about it. *What if they find out that I like this stuff?* This made *The Lord of the Rings* sound like some drug high school students try and need to hide from their parents. Well, if *LOTR* is indeed a drug, then, by all means, please distribute this one freely.

My initial thought was *"Whoa!"* Then, like magic, I felt the hole in my heart seal shut. Never once have I looked back and regretted *The Lord of the Rings* making its way to me. Before I would have never admitted the following to anyone, but even with all my attempts to fit in, I felt there was something more, something important that I was missing. Thus it was that, in my belief, Ilúvatar intervened and said, "Listen to me — *this* is what you need."

From that day forward, there was a bounce in my step. My disposition was changed; I had such joy in my heart that I could never fully explain it. I hungrily delved into Tolkien's other works, and found more satisfaction and love. From my previous state of doubt and pre-occupation with what I saw as the "damaged" areas in my life, I became the embodiment of a "life is good" campaign. My mother told me once (and she was only one of many who noted this change) that I now had this inner light shining brightly from within, and that this light drew and positively affected people. I like to think of that as my Eärendil light.

Now, as I do research and enthusiastically train to become a Tolkien scholar, many other opportunities have opened up for me. Pessimism and negativity are not options for me; instead, *LOTR* has taught me that a life of light and happiness in the elven spirit offers much more. Trusting that I play a part in a vast and ever-evolving tale makes me feel of great worth. Like Frodo and Sam, I also understand my role in the story is important and that my actions, both positive and negative, affect the other players. *I have a purpose.*

The Lord of the Rings is a gift, sent to the dreamers without lifejackets who are adrift in the sea of life. Those of us who dream are often seen as foolish and immature by others. But I must ask the naysayers: was not every great novelist, playwright, scientist, and inventor a dreamer to begin with? Is it so wrong, then, for us to envision something beyond modern mentality? I think not, and sense that Professor Tolkien would agree with me.

The Lord of the Rings can be a tool in mending the hurts of our wounded souls, but we cannot begin to heal without the desire to do so. Perhaps this is just what the world needs to help repair itself.

Or perhaps everyone just needs a hobbit.

Biography: Michelle Hillman. Michelle is currently a college sophomore, preparing to become a university professor of literature or history, with a side of linguistics. If she had her way, she would follow Professor Tolkien's lead and explore various fields of study. She hopes to live and teach in Scotland, spend her days opening the minds of youth to new worlds through literature, and become the professor that everyone wants to take a class from. In her free time, Shelly enjoys reading, studying, and making as many people laugh as she can.

All That's Green and Good
Gina Marie Walden

I was eight years old the very first time I questioned my faith. Every Sunday, my parents saw to it that my brothers and I attended church. After morning mass, all the children would run down the basement steps for our weekly catechism class.

Our instructor's chosen topic for one particular class was who gets to go to heaven. A fellow student had decided to inform those of us around him whom he thought could or would not be permitted into heaven. I was told that family pets and all other animals were not going to the Great Beyond. This upset me tremendously. I began to argue with my fellow Bible students and the instructor as well. This subject seemed to open up a floodgate of other questions. If God created the Garden of Eden, were the animals all kicked out along with Adam and Eve? If so, why wouldn't they be able to return? Are there flowers and trees in heaven? To have a love of nature at such a young age and not have those around you embrace that love was quite upsetting. Were there other people in the world who felt as I did?

During high school, several teachers had assigned *The Hobbit* as mandatory reading, or they would show the cartoon version to keep students occupied while they quietly graded papers. I never knew that there was so much more to this story, not until it came to movie theaters. There it was on the big screen: a story that has kings, Elves, Dwarves, Wizards and the never-ending battle between good and evil. What more could a 34-year-old ask for? The very next day at the public library, I asked for the rest of the story.

Lembas for the Soul

Several years and movies later, I wondered how this particular body of work had affected my life. Just as when I was a child, I began to question my surroundings. Only this time, I felt as if I had a few more answers for myself. Does nature speak to us? I believe it does. Why are we not listening to the Earth and all its creatures? Do we have anything comparable to the lurking evil emanating from the Fires of Isengard or Mordor? I am afraid we do. In reality, large corporations are devastating the world's rainforests and displacing its indigenous peoples. Vast global corporations have become the machine that's destroying all that's green and good in the world. *The Lord of the Rings* is a work of fiction — isn't it?

Not if all the rainforests are destroyed. How many more animals are to be placed on the endangered list? All these and many more questions come to mind. Then I realize that I am just one person and no one of great importance — just like the hobbits. So I have started on a small scale.

After reading *The Lord of the Rings*, I was inspired to make some changes in my own life. I began by participating in my first war protest. I joined Planned Parenthood in the fight for women's rights over their own bodies and have been working with several friends to get a local neighborhood food pantry up and running. In April 2005, a group of my friends and I attended a weekend wilderness training course. I am now able to make a fire without matches and can identify several local edible plants and wild flowers. Every day, I take the time to get in touch with nature. My backyard now has an array of herbs, flowers, and vegetables growing in it. Next year, I will attend Missouri State University's Master Gardener program. I want to learn all I can about gardening and hope to share this knowledge with others.

These are all small things compared to the big picture. When I think of the Earth becoming scorched and barren like Mordor — without vegetables, flowers, plants or trees — I think there should be more people working to protect the natural world and all its inhabitants.

Lembas For the Soul

The Lord of the Rings embraces many things everyday society has forgotten or disregarded. Tolkien reminds us that friends and family should be held in the highest esteem, that a man's word is one that should be kept, and women are warriors in their own right. Magic is real and everything in nature speaks to you, even the trees. All you need to do is embrace the natural world and take the time to listen. Have patience, for it's slow in coming. Just like the Ents.

Biography: Gina Marie Walden. Gina Marie resides in southwest Missouri with her husband, 12-year-old son, four cats and three dogs. Their home is appropriately dubbed *Waldabeast Village*. She is currently experiencing the joy and the terror of working on her first novel.

Lembas For the Soul

Up on the Roof
Andrea Ball

Remember the old James Taylor song "Up On The Roof"? "…on the roof's the only place I know …where you just have to wish to make it so…." That song always takes me back to being a 12-year-old sitting on the roof of our house in Iran, reading *The Lord of the Rings*. While kids in the United States were experiencing *Star Wars* at the movies, I was adjusting to life in a strange new country where not much of the outside world was allowed to infiltrate. I went to Tehran American School and had friends there, but apart from school, we couldn't spend much time together elsewhere.

In my quest for something to do, I discovered I could scramble from our second-story balcony up the neighbor's roof and jump over to the flat top of our own roof. I would sit in the shade of an air conditioning hut and read out loud to the wild cats living up there. Of course, I read them my favorite story, which just happened to be rather a long one. Since we were spending so much time together, I started bringing food to two kittens; they became my closest friends during that time! It seemed like Middle-earth came alive in a special way and the loneliness of my year in Iran was eased considerably by the fellowship found in the pages of *The Lord of the Rings*.

Reading aloud in that unusual sanctuary, I could envision and laugh at Frodo's dumb-founded expression in "A Conspiracy Unmasked." I could hear the songs at The Prancing Pony, as well as the shrieks of the relentless Nazgul. I shivered as the Witch King stepped into the broken gateway of Minas Tirith. Tolkien's description of Lothlorien, and especially the characters' reactions at Cerin Amroth, imparted to me an insight to our own

53

eternal souls in a timeless paradise. Just as a part of Frodo, the wanderer from The Shire, would remain there, a part of me has always remained up on the roof, being inspired by themes of friendship, self-sacrifice, and hope. I felt those noble traits in the characters might also be mine: I could be brave, loyal, determined, discerning, wise, and make a difference in the world.

As time went on, I found special friends who shared a passion for the story. My sister had gotten me started by reading me *The Hobbit* when I was seven years old. Our family traveled a bit, and everywhere we went, my sister and I would imagine hobbits hiding behind trees or Elves passing under starry nights. During high school years, my best friend and I would meet before school and talk about our favorite parts and write poetry.

Eleven years after leaving Iran, I was reading the books aloud again — this time to my most special friend, my husband — on our honeymoon in Yosemite. The forests there were a great place to read and imagine it was all happening around us. My husband, Steve, loved the adventure and especially the end when the hobbits return to the Shire as seasoned soldiers and rout out the ruffians. (He still wishes *The Scouring of The Shire* had been included in the films.) His favorite character is Aragorn, because of his humility and willingness to serve others. Like Aragorn, Steve is a loyal friend who is protective and self-sacrificing.

I always loved Boromir, who wasn't evil ... just foolish, as we all can be. He thought there could be some compromise and let his desire consume him. It was really beautiful when, realizing his folly, he fought to his death protecting Merry and Pippin. I think the movie version did tremendous justice to that scene. No matter how many times I read it or see it, I always cry.

Speaking of the movie, when I heard there was to be a film version of the books, I was frustrated and a little upset. No one should try to portray that incredibly unique story and world — it would ruin it for the imagination. However, when I finally saw a preview for *The Fellowship of the Ring*, I felt so excited! Everything was *exactly* as I had imagined it — maybe this movie thing would work out!

54

Lembas for the Soul

After the movies came out, an amazing thing happened — new fans were born! I found myself discussing characters and themes with the junior high kids I tutor in literature. My sister-in-law, Nancy, had never read the books, but loved the movies. Subsequently, she delved into the books and we spent hours going back and forth about our favorite parts and the differences between the books and movies. We totally bonded and are now much closer than we ever were before.

We had a big family outing to see the premiere of *The Return of the King* two weeks before it came out in theaters. Most of my family rang in the New Year 2005 by watching all the extended DVD editions of the movies. When we attended *The Lord of the Rings Symphony* at the Hollywood Bowl, a curious thing happened. As we were sitting under the stars, a huge moth flew out of the night right towards us and passed just over our heads. Nancy looked at me in surprise, then half-asked and half-exclaimed, "The eagles are coming!"

The good times and great discussions inspired by *The Lord of the Rings* can only come from a story that touches hearts in a very real way. Tolkien had a deep understanding of the hearts of people who desired hope in a fallen world. Reflecting on the themes of *LOTR*, I am reminded we each have a battle or burden every day, but life is far from hopeless. I am not a particularly wise or brave person. Most of us are not; we are more like hobbits. But I press on with the hope that a small person simply doing his part — whether that is to stand forth and say, "I'll do it," or to be a loyal supporter to another person — does make a difference. Then, like Frodo and Sam, we too can soar on the wings of eagles.

Biography: Andrea Ball. "I live in California now and am a wife and mother. I tutor junior high kids in literature and grammar. As I home school my daughter, I look forward to the day when we will read *The Lord of the Rings* together!"

Lembas for the Soul

Magic in Middle-earth
Chris B. Papineau

One of the most stunning achievements in the history of literature is *The Lord of the Rings* trilogy — and with the eleven Oscars won by *The Return of the King* in 2004, Tolkien's saga has become no less of a masterpiece of the film medium.

While this has been the subject of abundant news coverage worldwide, for me there is a very grass roots connection to this epic in my own hometown of Dedham, Massachusetts, just south of Boston. This is the person of the late Jean Roberts, a longtime Dedham resident and English teacher at Oakdale Elementary School.

Our favorite teachers are the sort of people who remain a part of us throughout our lives. For many, there is that certain educator who stood out, who had a profound influence on forming who we would become and what we in turn would pass on to others. Mrs. Roberts, who passed away in December of 2000, was just such a teacher for me.

She was my homeroom and English teacher in the sixth grade, and above all she loved books and reading. I have two sons myself now, ages four and one, who are already lovers of books. This is partly due to my passing on to them what Mrs. Roberts imparted to me.

The Middle-earth connection comes through her "Hobbit Club", one the warmest memories of my formative years. Mrs. Roberts loved the works of J.R.R. Tolkien, felt they had tremendous educational value and burned with desire to share them with her students. Her Hobbit Club was an optional part of the Oakdale experience offered to her sixth-grade students. It met twice a week in the school library at seven in the morning before classes started. She actually held two separate groups to accommodate all the interested students, so Mrs. Roberts arrived at work early four days a week for the entire school year.

Over the course of the year, we were assigned a chapter or two to read for each morning's session. We started with *The Hobbit*, then moved on to *The Lord of the Rings*. The morning meetings were devoted to discussion of the assigned chapters. In particular, I recall she assigned the *Council of Elrond* chapter twice, due to its complexity.

The mornings were not limited to discussions of the world of J.R.R. Tolkien. Mrs. Roberts insisted that we locate new vocabulary words in the reading assignments for each and every session and bring the definitions to the group. Additionally, she required that we identify figures of speech used in Tolkien's vivid descriptions: similes, metaphors, and personifications. My copies of the books — which I keep to this day — are marked with underlines of words such as "escarpment" and "victuals", and expressions such as "as thick as summer moths around a candle".

Aside from the Hobbit Club, which was above and beyond her normal duties as an English teacher, she ran a challenging sixth-grade reading curriculum. Book reports were due every two weeks, and she would never abide books which she believed were below a student's reading level. Her passion for the fantasy genre brought me not only to Middle-earth, but also to the worlds of C.S. Lewis, Lloyd Alexander, and Susan Cooper.

She extolled the virtues of avoiding television. She once stated she had watched a single program during the course of the year, that being coverage of the Pope's first visit to Boston. I'm certain she would not be pleased at the amount of time I spending watching the Boston Red Sox these days.

I also distinctly remember that she categorically detested film adaptations of books. She felt they spoiled her own mental picture of how the characters and imaginary lands appeared. I don't know how she would have felt about Peter Jackson's *The Lord of the Rings* adaptations, but no doubt she would have been disappointed that many peoples' only experience of Middle-earth would be through the films and never from the pages of Tolkien's books.

Her reverence for books was illustrated most vividly in one amusing mannerism: she would be beside herself at the sight of someone folding a book back while reading it. My copies of *The Lord of the Rings*, for all the wear they have had over the years, still lack the telltale creases on the bindings which made Mrs. Roberts wince.

Furthermore, I will never forget the spelling of words such as "necessary" and "receive", thanks to Mrs. Roberts' simple rhythmic memory devices: N-E-C-E-"DOUBLE S"-A-R-Y. This is typical of the sort of "bag of tricks" all gifted teachers seem to possess.

It is over a quarter of a century since I was a student of Jean Roberts, and life's path has brought me to a place which resembles Middle-earth in many ways: the shadow of the Rocky Mountains in Denver, Colorado. I have a family of my own there, although my mother and father still live in the same home just south of Boston.

But if I live to be eleventy-one, there will always be a way to Middle-earth through the Oakdale School library, born of the magic of Mrs. Jean Roberts. Like Tolkien's immortal Elves, she has sailed to her place of rest in the Far West, but her spirit will endure as I read *The Hobbit* to my own children at bedtime.

Biography: Chris B. Papineau. Chris is a software engineer, citizen of Boston Red Sox nation, *Star Wars* fan, and graduate of the Massachusetts Institute of Technology. He can often be found in the Rocky Mountains of Colorado, on skis or in a tent by a warm fire. His "Precious" is his wife Marija and his two boys, David and Marc. In whatever spare time work and family allow, he is quietly at work creating his own saga. Above all, he is grateful to God for a life full of all manner of blessings.

Keeper of Lost Tales
Alexandra L. Jobson

J.R.R. Tolkien and Peter Jackson have changed my life forever. They have enriched my life and changed my outlook on many things. Whenever I hear the theme to *The Lord of the Rings* or any of the music from these epics, I stop and try to find out where it is coming from. If I close my eyes and listen to the music of Howard Shore, I'm escorted to Middle-earth and lose all sense of the world I am really in. People have to tear me away.

The novels are something with which I can just crawl into bed and escape into. My dreams fill with the beauty of the Elves and their sweet music soothes my soul. Then I wake up and am disappointed it all wasn't real.

When I watch *The Lord of the Rings* movies at home, I go to my favorite parts with ethereal music and dance lightly around the floor, barely feeling the ground beneath me. I imagine myself an Elf, dancing in the forest, wearing a flowing dress, glowing like the sun, with the wind blowing through my hair. Howard Shore's music has instilled such images of beauty in my mind, I can't even begin to explain it. The song *The Grey Havens* makes me cry almost every time I hear it. I envision myself standing on a beach, the sea wind fresh in my face, as if I, too, was passing across the sea, never to return. I see myself wearing a bright white dress, and I feel very sad, but still calm, at peace.

These experiences have reshaped my desires about what I want to study and practice when I am older. I hope to study Tolkien's works in more detail in college. I now want to become an instructor at a college level to teach others about Tolkien and his works so that they will enjoy reading them as much as I do. I wish I could have met Tolkien; to meet such a genius would be an extreme honor.

One reason I love Tolkien's novels is because they don't apply to any specific time period. He wrote them so all generations can read them and decide what meaning the tales have in their own lives. They didn't have to live then to understand why he wrote them. One of the things that make these books so wonderful is that everyone can relate to them somehow.

I personally empathize with Éowyn. She wants to go to war, to fight, to be brave and valiant, but no one respects her desires. I have always wanted to be the one to fight and be brave, but since I am seen just as a naive girl, I have never had the chance to do it. I have always longed for a quest or journey, something new that will send me on my own grand adventure. But I can't — the world doesn't work like that anymore.

I'm the only one in school who really loves the movies and the books. I did a project on it to try to promote them, but everyone laughed at me. I want to share the beauty I have experienced and the wisdom I have gained, but not many feel the same way and it's very difficult to even begin to explain it to anyone. Believe me, I've tried!! I'll never understand why others don't have the same feelings I do. If there is one reader who is reading this now, and he or she understands how I feel and understands what I am saying, I'm glad I'm not the only one.

It's great to escape to *The Lord of the Rings* at night, knowing full well it isn't real, to leave this boring world behind for a place full of beauty, love, fantasy, bravery, loyalty and friendship. I wonder what it would be like to be in such an epic story. These stories are so wonderful I can't wait to share them with my children and grandchildren someday. I can only hope they'll enjoy them and treasure them as much as I have.

These stories and movies are just so beautiful and pure they've *changed my life forever*.

Thank you, John Ronald Reuel Tolkien, for giving us the incredible world of Middle-earth. And thank you, Peter Jackson, for making that world real and even more beautiful.

Lembas for the Soul

My Biography—*so far!:* Alexandra L. Jobson.
Grade: 8th
Age: 14
Favorite Movies: *The Lord of the Rings* of course!! *Star Wars* comes right behind.
Pets: Two silly cats: Cosmo and Socks, three fish and a hermit crab
Favorite Sports Team: Denver Broncos
Family: Mommy, Daddy, and little sister Mary-Elizabeth who's only nine
Favorite Sport: Volleyball, skim boarding, and am going to learn to surf soon
Favorite Actor: Viggo Mortensen, Hayden Christensen comes right after!
Favorite Actress: Liv Tyler

Legendarium as Lembas
Edie Head

I wasn't thinking about a spiritual experience when I picked up the three paperback volumes of *The Lord of the Rings* in the '60's. I had read *The Hobbit* to my children in 1963, and thought it quite the best children's book I had ever encountered. I was disappointed when the librarian said he hadn't written anything else (of course, she was wrong). But here were three books, no less, and I had read interesting things about them in the letter columns of the *New York Times'* book review section. I couldn't afford to buy many books back then, but the library didn't have them, and I decided to take the risk of buying all three. My husband was going out of town on business for a few days, and I needed something to read after the four kids were tucked into bed.

I ended up reading it day and night, with a baby on my hip, laying it down when I had to, reading until dawn. It took me four days. I was only thinking about the story; certainly not spirituality. I was a Unitarian, alienated from Christianity by my childhood church experiences and my reading in history; all I wanted was a good story. As a result, as Frodo and Sam struggled up Mount Doom in what seemed to be their futile attempt to destroy the Ring, I was amazed to find myself thinking that all God requires of us is to do the very best we can, and, if that isn't enough, Grace will get us through. Grace? Unitarians didn't talk about Grace!

The day after I finished the appendices, I started reading the books to my kids. For the only time in my parenting career, I had perfect kids: if they misbehaved, all I had to do was say "If you don't behave, I won't read tonight...." Once we had finished,

I never found anything else that worked like that! They, of course, were interested in the story, but I was noticing things I had missed in the first breakneck reading. About how things were *meant* to happen. About passages that, if there had been any religion in the book, would be called at least 'spiritual.'

I reread the books many times, as my life situation changed. I left the Unitarians when I decided that it was a great place for people who were sure what they *didn't* believe, but wasn't a good fit for me, as more and more, I began finding out what I *did* believe. I studied a great many spiritual traditions; first and always Native American, Taoism, Buddhism, Sufism, the *philosophia perennis*. I earned advanced degrees in Native American studies and in Transpersonal Psychology (that branch of psychology that deals with the interface between psychology and spirituality). And every time I reread Tolkien, I found more hints of the things I was coming to believe about our human dealings with the Divine.

When I read *about* Tolkien, I discovered his own spiritual path, a Roman Catholic orthodoxy that was impossible for me, even though I had ended up in the Episcopal Church. I was convinced that the spirituality I found permeating his pages was no accident. Then why, I asked myself, was there no religion in Middle-earth? I knew enough about anthropology and history to know that there has never been a culture without some way to deal with humanity's innate spirituality. Tolkien was a student of history and of early European cultures, as well as being a deeply religious man; surely he, of all people, knew that his portrait of Middle-earth was lacking one of the universal elements of human culture. Why? What was going on here?

The first clue I got was my realization that Tolkien revered the anonymous Beowulf Poet, and that he saw himself as doing in the 20th century what the Poet had done in his own time. The Poet was a Christian who was reworking the pre-Christian stories of his people into a poem that would entertain and sustain those people in their new Christian life. He was an honest man, who knew that the stories he was retelling were about people who had never heard of Christ. He could not do violence to those stories by falsifying them with an unhistorical Christianity. But he, as a good Christian, could not include in his retelling the pagan religious beliefs and practices which had been part of the original stories. So he left them out. And he didn't replace them with anything; just left a hole in the stories where paganism once was.

And that is precisely what Tolkien did with Middle-earth.

Tolkien was writing an epic based on many, many things; the languages he loved (both existing and imagined), the mythology he believed his beloved England had been deprived of by the brutal Norman conquest, the passionate devotion of his faithful heart to the values both of the heroic Northern world and of Christianity. His legendarium consumed him, filled his thoughts and his dreams, kept him sane at the Somme and after.

It developed from his first attempts at writing it down in 1914 on to the very end of his long life. And, I believe, he took as his role model the Beowulf Poet. He would not introduce Christianity into a world millennia older than Christ. But neither would he write about, and in so doing, glorify, any other religion. So, he left it out. He left us to believe, if we wanted to, that the only religion that ever existed in Middle-earth was the abomination of Sauron-worship.

You can believe that, if you want to, but I don't want to. I prefer to believe that the cultures of Middle-earth were like all other cultures that have ever existed everywhere on Earth. They had mythology, and mythology does not exist without a religious world view. They had values and cultural norms that *had* to have had some kind of religious sanction. The Valar are clearly gods, in the tradition of pre-Christian European gods, and Iluvatar is clearly *God,* the Creator and Ground of Being. Middle-earth in the first Four Ages was not, uniquely in the world, without some form of religion.

And now for the fun part. If the cultures of Middle-earth had religions, what were they like? There are, of course, many clues in the books. When you start looking for them, they just pop out at you. Trying to reconstruct them is like doing Biblical criticism; I try to stay absolutely grounded in the texts and in what I know of human nature and religiosity. I try, in other words, to be an honest scholar. My reconstructions are based in my love of Tolkien and my determination to be true to the letter of his works as well as the spirit. And so —

The religion of the Shire I think of as combining Celtic and Anglo-Saxon elements, very much earth-based and tied to the agricultural round. Maypoles and sacred springs, a little sex magic in the fields at sowing and harvest times. Lots of singing and dancing and feasting, confused memories of elvish mythology (surely Bilbo and Frodo were not the only Elf Friends in hobbit history), lots of half-remembered stories of the hobbit migrations. Some stories explaining the iffy relationships of hobbits and the other speaking races. Farmer Maggot was in close contact with Tom Bombadil, so surely some knowledge of Tom and barrow wights, and the Old Forest would have been included in the stories told round the hearth fires at night.

The Elves had their memories of The Western Lands, and their own tragic history. They had the advantage of being immortal, so there were always Elves around who remembered the happenings of the earlier Ages. Those memories and their immortality, it seems to me, would result in a religion with strong Buddhist elements. Compassion for all sentient beings (orcs not included), meditation in an effort to renew the sorely regretted lost relationship with the Valar, and Iluvatar beyond. Devotion to Elbereth Gilthoniel, a special reverence for the stars. The type of Buddhism that uses gods and goddesses as metaphors and foci of devotion.

The religion in Beorn's territories must have been much like several Native American groups who knew the reality of beings who moved back and forth between animal and human. The Gondorians practiced some kind of ancestor worship (like Confucianism?), and the Rohirrim, of course, practiced the lost religion of the Anglo Saxons.

I have enjoyed this game; it brings me closer to Tolkien's world, strengthens my faith in the reality of his legendarium, gives me courage for the journey, and makes me happy. What more could I ask of *lembas*?

Lembas does for the physical body what mythology does for the soul. Tolkien was, as much as a philologist, a mythographer. He understood the importance of myth for the human psyche. He was one of those Europeans for whom the traditional Judaeo-Christian mythology had not lost its ability to function in the nurturing of the soul. But for many, as Joseph Campbell notes, the old biblical stories have lost that ability. The demand of many of our churches that the stories be taken as factual history has destroyed their ability to work for us as archetypal and metaphorical truth. We are left alone in a cold, unfriendly world, hungry for meaning, desperate for help for on the journey. We need Gandalf. We need *lembas* for the soul.

When hard-core Tolkien fans get together, one of the first things they do is ask, "What character do you relate to?" The first time I was asked that, I said, "I'm the Lady in Beorn's hall." "But there was no lady in Beorn's hall!" "Oh yes, there was; she just didn't get into the book." With my passion for Native American ways, and my life-long identification with Bear Power, Beorn was a natural for me. And that is the mark of a true mythology; it is powerful and spacious, it has archetypes to which everyone can relate, it provides nourishment for the journey, heroes to try to live up to, values to guide your life decisions. It has to be alive in your heart, or it can't sustain you as you struggle up your own Mount Doom.

Tolkien's Middle-earth is alive for many of us in a way that Eden is not. Gandalf and Aragorn give us the role models that Abraham and David don't. Those who never knew the Virgin Mary find her in Galadriel or Elbereth. Would Tolkien be horrified at this development, or would he be quietly pleased that he had found a way to sneak the traditional Christian values back into the popular culture of our time? We will never know. But I like to think he would not be upset. After all, he invented *lembas*.

Lembas for the Soul

Biography: Edie Head. "I was born a Californian, married a New Englander and raised my family in Massachusetts, have lived for extended periods in Oklahoma (twice) and Utah, and am now happily retired in Virginia. I have been a homemaker, chef, social worker and costumed interpreter in a living history Indian museum. I discovered Tolkien in 1964, looking in the local library for something to read to my kids. The kids loved *The Hobbit* and soon thereafter *The Lord of the Rings,* and I fell in love with Tolkien, and have never stopped reading him. (I'm halfway through *The History of Middle-earth* at present; this is my second reading. That's devotion.) When I decide I need to read *LOTR* again, I start with *The Silmarillion* and *The Hobbit.* I love Tolkien for so many reasons; I'll never forget the anguished feeling when I finished *LOTR* the first time, that it was over and I was shut out of the Garden. Fortunately, I found my way back, again and again.

Tolkien's writings, Jackson's movies, the sound tracks, *the OneRing.net*, my online friendships with fellow Tolkienists (I am a charter member of The Order of the Venerable Saint Viggo) fill my days (and nights) with joy. Like Howard Shore, I don't want to leave Middle-earth, and I'm getting pretty good at staying there. In addition to beautiful writing, a magical setting, mythic characters, one of Tolkien's greatest attractions for me is the reverence for God and Creation that permeates his work. The values his characters embody, the faith in ultimate goodness that Gandalf quietly spreads in the midst of death and despair, nourish my own faith that all shall be well, all shall be well, all manner of things shall be well."

Lessons from Heroes
Karen Dennen

When my husband first told me he was going to see *The Fellowship of the Ring,* I said I didn't like fantasy and wished him a good time.

That was three movies ago. By the time *The Two Towers* came out, I'd heard so many strong, positive reactions to the first movie, I decided perhaps I'd better watch *The Fellowship* quickly if I intended to see *The Two Towers.*

Afterward, when I had become completely captivated by the first two films, we found ourselves asking what it is about *The Lord of the Rings* that sets it apart from other fantasy fiction, especially in the eyes of women. The legions of *Star Trek* fans include a much smaller percentage of women than men, after all.

Perhaps the key lies in the men of the Fellowship, as much as in Peter Jackson's interpretation of the women. There are nine wonderful role models who are all variations on a theme, extensions of one soul bound by a common mission, united by the Ring. Each character embodies a quality both men and women seek. Their behavior sets an example of nobility and courage for the rest of us. With a bit of effort we could be any of them — or, if we're lucky, married to a man who aspires to those ideals.

We can find parallels from high school as comparisons. Gimli is the short, chubby guy who impressed us with his sincerity and humility. He dares not ask anything but to gaze upon Galadriel, whom he once mistrusted. As he takes his last look, he requests a strand of hair, but is granted three. For him, it's reward enough.

Lembas for the Soul

Legolas is the best friend from high school. His unflinching loyalty compels him to bring a Dwarf into the land of the Elves, where he risks alienating his own people. He watches the rest of his race go into the West, but will not leave Aragorn's side.

Frodo is the essence of determination and selflessness. He's the guy who got all the answers correct on the test, but wouldn't give you the answers if you tried to cheat off his paper. His honest, virtuous nature reinforces his desire to resist temptation, even if in the end he doesn't entirely succeed.

Merry and Pippin are the class clowns who make us laugh. Threatening to no one, their growth through adversity astounds even themselves, and they surprise us — and themselves — with their courage. Beneath their comic exteriors we always sense that, if necessary, they can reach into themselves and find more than they believe they are capable of.

Sam is the soul of loyalty. He stays by Frodo no matter what the risk, even when his best friend temporarily loses faith in him. In the end, because he is so deserving, he gets the girl of his dreams. There's a depth to Sam no one could imagine early on in the films.

Aragorn is captain of the football team, the straight-A student who is king of the senior prom and first pick for Harvard. Humble and unassuming, he is the essence of the romantic hero and what all men strive to be, or should.

With the wisdom and grace of age, Gandalf is the history teacher who has learned from the past. The voice of authority and dignity, he is the one to whom everyone turns for comfort, advice, and inspiration. He knows better than anyone that sometimes we must stand up and take charge, even if it is not in the original plan, and that it is how we spend our allotted time that counts.

With his passion, nobility, and courage, Boromir is the lineman ejected from the game for his temper, who still believes he was justified. He is the bad boy parents don't want their daughter to date, the guy in the torn T-shirt with cigarettes tucked in his sleeve.

Lembas for the Soul

Despite his dark side, the story turns bittersweet with the loss of Boromir. Just as he looks into the snowstorm and predicts it will be the death of the hobbits if they continue, there are always some who don't survive the journey. Even at the end of the quest, when Frodo is safe, the ring destroyed, and Aragorn crowned king, the joy shared by the eight who are left is tempered by the loss of their Gondorian comrade. In life's delicate balance, joy is always tempered by loss. The same is true of our lives.

It is when facing their worst crisis that the men of the Fellowship rise to the challenge. We can learn from their example, taking to heart their responses to fear and danger. Like invisible friends, they walk with us. I sometimes ask myself how Legolas would handle a given situation. Can my wisdom rise to Gandalf's level? If Frodo can take on his monumental calling, whatever task I face seems easy by comparison.

After a particularly difficult stretch in my life, a friend reminded me that what doesn't kill us makes us stronger. Today when I hear that advice, I think of Gimli, motivated to seek justice by the loss of Balin and others of the Dwarf race.

Had we been in high school together, we women could have had a crush on all of them. (Many of us still do.) We aren't so different, after all. We are all travelers on the same path, mariners seeking our way to safety on the high seas. During times of adversity, we should ask ourselves with whom we identify. Have we the presence of mind of Eowyn, or the courage of our convictions like Arwen? Are we more like Aragorn or Pippin?

Even Pippin's impulsive instincts are altered along the way by circumstance. His true courage emerges when he faces the ultimate test. Do we have the courage to lead the way to explore the Paths of the Dead as Aragorn did, or would we go around? Like Aragorn summoning the only army he can, full of noble purpose, we'd all love to be able to follow in his footsteps.

Whether we find life magic or tragic, we can ease our way by looking to heroes for guidance. We, too, must make it our quest to fight the good fight. The lessons we can learn from characters in *The Lord of the Rings* extend beyond the Fellowship.

Denethor teaches us we shouldn't wait too long to appreciate our children. We can look to Arwen and Eowyn as examples of feminine bravery combined with grace and integrity. In Tolkien's school, it's how we respond to life that makes us different and defines our essence — what we do with the time given to us, Gandalf would tell us.

For those seeking a light in dark places, even when grief and turmoil threaten to distract us from our purpose, the light of the Fellowship shines like a beacon across the peaks and valleys of our lives.

Biography: Karen Dennen. Karen lives on the East Coast with her husband, two daughters, and an assortment of pets. A writer and artist, she volunteered for many years, writing "Pet of the Month" newspaper columns and hosting *Pet Talk*, a cable TV interview show for a local pet welfare organization. Among her heroes are numerous deceased authors including Dickens and Emerson, her husband, who proposed marriage onstage at a Renaissance fair, and, of course, the members of the Fellowship.

The Light of Eärendil

The Light of Eärendil

A Light in Dark Places

The American Hobbit Association
Renee Alper

It all started in the 1960s with those book-ordering companies in school. I ordered everything that wasn't sports or romance (yech!). So, it was inevitable that one day I would come home with a copy of *The Fellowship of the Ring*. "Cool book," my older brother said, "but it's part of a series. You have to read *The Hobbit* first." He tossed a coverless, torn book onto my bed and walked out. I resented his opinion, but took his advice.

I spent the rest of the fifth grade and most of the sixth reading *The Hobbit* and *The Lord of the Rings*. Every recess, break, and after homework, I was journeying with Bilbo, aching for Frodo and mooning over Aragorn. I savored each part. When Strider and the hobbits stopped on Weathertop, shadows seemed to loom in every dark corner of my room. I cheered first at *The Departure of Boromir*, and then wept at my hasty judgment of a good man. And I felt every burdened step of Frodo's last days in Mordor. Middle-earth had become my home.

Soon after beginning college, I developed severe arthritis and was forced to drop out. I spent a year and a half doing *nothing*, an almost impossible task for an overachiever like myself. Then, in 1977, I read a small notice that changed my life forever. The Mythopoeic Society (a fan club for Tolkien and other fantasy authors) announced a new Tolkien sub-group was forming in the Chicago area. I volunteered to assist and became one of the co-founders of *Minas Aearon* (Tower by the Great Sea, a reference to the John Hancock Building or the Sears Tower) and editor of its newsletter, *Annuminas* (West Tower).

This was a great boon to me since, as my illness progressed, I was unable to go back to college or get a job. Although I needed a wheelchair and had limited use of my hands, I typed the newsletter every month, able to use only two fingers (long before the days of home computers). I corrected every typo, re-threading the paper to match the previously typed text. It was a painstaking labor of love, and it showed.

I was soon Chief Everything, doing everything from meeting planning to newsletter publishing to recruiting to fundraising to ... well, you name it. I put free announcements in the local community newspaper, which led to feature articles in all three major Chicago papers. Our membership grew quite significantly.

We reached international status by our second year, and I changed the group's name to The American Hobbit Association to reflect this. Its acronym was AHA; "Aha" is the Elvish word for "rage", and we were the 'rage' of the country! I renamed the newsletter *The Rivendell Review*, as my character in the group was Arwen. Rivendell was also the nickname for my family's house and our meeting place.

We got rave reviews from other Tolkien clubs and books. Our membership exceeded 200, which, without the help of the internet, was a lot of people. Our meetings could exceed 40 guests, and ranged from book discussions to gaming to costume parties. We attended Bakshi's movie version of *LOTR* and Renaissance Faires in full gear: cloaks, swords, long dresses, and all. We even visited a restaurant which served Bilbo Burgers!

Our biggest events were our annual costumed fundraiser, The Midsummer Faire and Auction, our Hobbit Dinner, a recreation of Bilbo's Long-Expected Party, with mushrooms, *lembas*, and even a Great Cake (from Tolkien's *Smith of Wootten Major*). We were the biggest solely-Tolkien, fully operational – having both meetings and a newsletter – club in the Western Hemisphere.

Lembas for the Soul

It was exciting to think that all over the world, people were reading and enjoying my publication, which grew from a two-page bulletin to a full-fledged fanzine, complete with cover art, regular columns, Middle-earth stories, non-fiction articles, puzzles, and jokes. Members would write letters for our letters column, telling me how much they loved the club, and how they would wait anxiously for the next issue to appear in their mailbox!

At the 1982 World Science Fiction Convention in Chicago, AHA members performed an original play, *The Greatest Gondorian Hero*, a parody of the TV show, *The Greatest American Hero*, set in Middle-earth. We also published *The Tales of Aragorn and Arwen*, a fanzine containing short stories, artwork, poetry, and songs about the royal couple, including two stories by Marion Zimmer Bradley (author of the *Darkover* series and *The Mists of Avalon*)!

In 1986, I moved to Cincinnati, Ohio, still in a wheelchair. Shortly after the move, my neck was broken in a car accident. I put out the issue that was on the boards at the time, and folded shop. For nearly 12 years, *The Hobbit* and *The Lord of the Rings* had been my passion, my profession and my art. In founding *The American Hobbit Association*, I created a legacy in tribute to this great author. The publications that passed through my typewriter, and later my printer, remain on file in the Wade Collection, an Inklings library in Wheaton, IL, and at Marquette University in Milwaukee, Wisconsin, the home of the original manuscripts of Tolkien's works.

My life as the heartbeat of the AHA has changed me, all for the better. Some of my friends today, I met through the AHA. I consider myself a seasoned editor and am totally undaunted by the prospect of a cold telephone call. Through my fame and experience with the AHA, I had the opportunity to be the Dramaturg for a three-year, three-part Cincinnati production of *The Lord of the Rings*.

Although we have gone our separate ways, many of the members of the AHA remain in touch. We even have an annual reunion at a Chicago-based science fiction/fantasy convention!

The American Hobbit Association remains one of the major accomplishments of my life, and it and its members will always hold a special place in my heart.

Biography: Renee Alper. Renee founded The American Hobbit Association in 1977, which she ran until 1989. She also performs music with her partner, Ray Phoenix, in their singer/songwriter duo, "A Little R&R". An actress, director and playwright, she also served as Dramaturg for a three-part, three-year production of *The Lord of the Rings*, adapted for the stage by Blake Bowden. She starred in and directed her play, "Roll Model", about a disability support group (she is disabled and uses a motorized wheelchair). Other writing accomplishments include several produced plays, and current projects include an autobiographical play and a book of humorous quotes from job applicants.

Walking With Hobbits

AJ Caywood

By the winter of 2001, I had reached the lowest point of my adult life. In 1995, I survived a head-on collision that almost killed me, crushing me from the waist down and leaving me with the possibility I may never walk again. I had two young daughters to raise. I struggled to heal and after a whole year, I began to walk on my own again. Even though I had reached this milestone, I had to accept the fact that constant pain, limited mobility, and multiple surgeries would always be a part of my future.

Three years later, in the summer of 1998, just when I thought my life was getting back on track, another devastating blow struck my family. My mother-in-law, two sisters-in-law, and 11-year-old niece were killed together in a car accident when a woman who was speeding ran a red light and hit them. A third sister-in-law, the fifth passenger in the vehicle, was the only survivor. Ironically, this family member was the most fragile of the five, as she was mentally, physically, and emotionally handicapped from birth. It was a miracle she grew into adulthood; another miracle that she survived this horrible crash. Our large family was now only a shattered remnant of its former self.

Trying to make sense of this astounding loss, console and care for my children, husband and other family members, plus finding a way to grieve for four people at once, stripped me clean emotionally. A year and a half to the day of the accident that took so many from us, my father-in-law suddenly passed away from a massive heart attack. This left his adult handicapped daughter alone. Her older brother and I took turns trying to care for her 24/7 for the next eight months. A month after my father-in-law passed away, my own father told me the horrific news that he had aggressive lung cancer. While my father lay in the hospital, recuperating from an unsuccessful lung surgery, my grandmother passed away. Eleven months later, my father lost his battle with cancer and my mother had to bury her husband on their 26th wedding anniversary.

Just as the burden of the Ring weighed on Frodo, layer after heavy layer of depression slowly smothered my soul. I fought to stay one step ahead of the wave of overwhelming grief and loss. One of the things I did to escape was to lose myself for an hour or so in a movie. We went to the movies a lot during this time, and there were a few whose stories soothed an aching heart and began to coax the light back into my life.

On a cold winter evening, my husband, two daughters and I went to the theater to see a new fantasy movie that critics were raving about. The title was familiar to me, but I'd never read the books. For the next few hours, I was transported into a magical world of sights, sounds and emotions. As the credits rolled, the lights blinked on and I rose from my seat, my mind swirled with a myriad of thoughts and feelings. I had just watched *The Fellowship of the Ring*.

From that moment on, I knew Middle-earth would always have a special place in my heart, touching me deeply during a terrible time in my life. I was a voracious reader while in school and couldn't figure out how I'd missed this story. That week, I purchased the trilogy and immersed myself in Tolkien's world. I was not the only one in my household whom the movie had affected; my two daughters fell in love with it as well.

My car accident in 1995 left me with limited mobility in my knee and ankle joints, cutting many things I used to be able to do out of my life and out of my children's lives. Our love of *The Lord of the Rings* brought us closer, bonding us tighter as mother and daughters. The three of us discussed the story, themes and characters, got online and researched websites for any juicy morsel of news. We anxiously awaited the next two movies. We would sit on the bed at night, each of us taking turns reading the story aloud. We had our favorite characters, cheering them on through their adventures. Through this experience, we were able to make memories that will last a lifetime.

When *The Two Towers* hit theaters, my love for this story helped ignite a long-buried aspiration of mine to become a writer. Tolkien's magnificent literary work and Peter Jackson's amazing visual portrayal sparked the creative part of my soul. Passion for a long-lost dream burned through me, and I began to pursue this personal goal. In January of 2004, my revived dream was realized when my very first manuscript was accepted for publication. Although there were other factors that encouraged me to chase my dream, I consider *The Lord of the Rings* a major influence and inspiration.

Since I am a dreamer at heart, I found myself totally caught up in this epic tale. I thought of the hobbits, a wizard, a Ranger, Elves, a Dwarf and the peoples of Gondor and Rohan as friends. Reading about and watching these special characters struggle mightily against all odds made me feel as if I wasn't so alone. I followed them along on their quest, walking with the hobbits and learning to find my way through my own mist and shadow.

As Aragorn accepted the challenge set before him in *The Return of the King*, I accepted the challenges in my life. I plowed on, with my friends from Middle-earth in my heart, pushing through the pain and realizing I could still find light in my life. Ultimately, I attribute three things that gave me the strength and courage to find myself where I am today: my faith in God, my family — especially my children, who looked to me for guidance — and the connection I found with *The Lord of the Rings*. I have deep appreciation and gratitude for Tolkien, who brought this work of genius to life upon the pages; and for Peter Jackson, and his dedicated cast and crew, who brought it to life on the big screen. I do not believe my life would be the same without having this literary and cinematic experience to enrich my life.

I had no say in those tragic events that changed my life so dramatically. As a wise old wizard once said, only I can decide what to do with the time I'd been given. These words resonated inside me time and time again, encouraging me to push through the darkness and bring light back into my life. I knew that my old life was nothing but a whisper, a mere remnant of who I used to be. I'd never be able to pick up where I left off; too many people had been ripped away, too many things had changed. *The Lord of the Rings* entered my life during a time when I desperately needed it, penetrating the thick swath of depression. It gave me *hope*. I found my courage again, leaned harder on my faith, and reached out to friends to help me carry the load.

At a crossroads in the journey of my life, I paused for a moment in Middle-earth and met its unforgettable inhabitants. Their journey of courage, love, strength, and friendship inspired me to search for the happiness I thought I'd never have again. I keep going because there is still good in this world, and when I reach the end of my path, I'll smile, knowing I did the most with the time I'd been given.

Biography: AJ Caywood. AJ grew up reading C.S. Lewis, Robin McKinley, Madeleine L'Engle, and Walter Farley. It wasn't until she became an adult that she found the amazing world of J.R.R. Tolkien's *The Lord of the Rings*, which is now one of her favorite books and movies. AJ's love of the written word led her to pursue her dream of becoming an author herself, and in 2004, her first novel and a short story were published. Her author website is www.AJCaywood.com. She lives in central Kentucky with her husband and two daughters.

Lembas for the Soul

Galadriel's Phial
Lauren Nowalski

At their parting in *The Fellowship of the Ring*, Galadriel gave Frodo a phial full of the light of their most blessed elven star. It was to illuminate the darkest of places on Frodo's journey. The phial helped Frodo in Shelob's lair, then Sam when he searched for Frodo in the orc tower. The light put them in mind of the unsullied woods of Lorien and the fairness of Rivendell. It reminded them of the goodness and purity they were fighting for, even if they could not dwell there. All this was from the shining brilliance of a little star glass.

I was about six years old when I received *The Lord of the Rings* boxed set from a neighbor. She was extremely intellectual and knew the books had been highly acclaimed. I was a ravenous reader by the age of six and loved to read almost anything. My eyes grew wide as I read and saw the rushing waters of Rivendell, the timeless Golden Wood and the lush beauty of the Shire. When Frodo stood in the heart of Mount Doom, I could feel the heat stinging my eyes as if I was really there. I could disappear into my own little universe — my private, portable magic carpet to a whole new world.

When I was in the hospital at age seven, I was quite frightened of my planned surgery. Once again, my wonderful *Lord of the Rings* books saved me. It made the stay in the hospital much more bearable. Lying in a sanatorium bed was of no concern to me; how could it be, when I rode with the Rohirrim to the wars of Gondor?

These books inspired me; they were my guiding light. When I was a child and my parents fought, I could go up to my room and enjoy myself in peaceful Hobbiton, safely away from it all. The screaming would melt away as the dialogue of Frodo and Sam blocked it out. In school, I used Tolkien's ideas as a base for my own stories. I was always the one who had the ideas, the imagination and the big thoughts. I taught the other children to "make pretend", inspired by the far-off worlds Tolkien once imagined. I read the books for strength and comfort when I felt depressed; when my parents got divorced, when the other children mocked and ridiculed me, Frodo became my friend and companion.

The Lord of the Rings eventually inspired me to write my own stories. I created far-off worlds just for myself: vast universes from my own brain, worlds that changed according to my rules, my wants, my needs. Of course, this kind of life-shirking couldn't continue my whole life, and it definitely didn't. I made friends, took on responsibilities, once again becoming part of the world outside my books. Some of my friends were quite interested in *The Lord of the Rings*, others were not. But that was just fine with me.

The books could also be my enemy as well. I received immeasurable amounts of teasing and taunting because of my interest in Middle-earth. When we were told to give our math binders a theme, mine was *The Lord of the Rings*; on the front, a full color picture of the One Ring against a background of flames, the seven rings surrounding it, with a border of dwarven runes. Each new section had a character on its introduction page. I was so proud of it! The other children made fun of me, mocking it, but I received an A-plus. What did it matter to me if the other children didn't like it? It was for my enjoyment alone!

Of course, I found other interests: math, science, art, and music. But I still kept Middle-earth in my heart; it nurtured my imagination and led me to literature and writing stories.

The Lord of the Rings was like my bible through my growing years; but it was also more than that. It helped me overcome crippling anxiety, countless depressing situations, and it even gave me the inspiration to start writing stories. It taught me my first lessons of humanity, courage, duty, the importance of friendship and trust, and that good is always worth fighting for, in a literal or metaphorical sense. There is always hope, a way to achieve your ends. Evil is not always cut and dry. These I learned, too. The books taught me the value of compassion, that there *can* be worse fates than death. And finally, what seems right sometimes can only be obtained through sacrifice.

The books were an important part of my education; they taught me all the lessons a woman can learn from life. They were my shining stars, my guiding lights, my star in the darkness, when all other lights went out. They were my Galadriel's phial.

Biography: Lauren Nowalski. When Lauren is not in Middle-earth she is playing the piano, singing, acting, reading or writing. She also is infatuated with languages and the sciences. She is currently independently learning Japanese, French, Spanish and Latin, and hopes to aim for Hindi. She is trying to find ways to save people with her pen while aiding the environment. She hopes to eventually hold a job in solar power while continuing to write. She also privately aspires to be poet laureate.

A Far Green Country

I first saw *The Lord of the Rings: The Fellowship of the Ring* when I was only 11 years old. Two years later, when I saw *The Return of the King*, the song *Into the West* really struck a chord within me. I also heard Gandalf say, "End? No, the journey doesn't end here. Death is just another path, one that we must all take."

Shortly after that, I learned my uncle was diagnosed with cancer. When he passed away and I attended his services, *Into the West* was playing over and over in my head. I could barely hear the preacher talking about my uncle. I could just picture him beyond the sea, in "a far green country under a swift sunrise."

The Lord of the Rings has lit a fire within me that cannot be put out. The books and movies have inspired me to live as a better person. They have taught me that when I make my own way into the West to those white shores, I should not be afraid.

Katie Perkins

Hope Again
O. Rivera

The last five years have been really difficult financially, physically and emotionally. While in hindsight, I can see the progress of my life, it has been slow, painful and at times, discouraging. However, I had never lost hope, not until this year.

This year started with huge plans. We planned to buy a house, to change our settings, to find new and better jobs ... and the list goes on. I knew my life felt very disordered, and that it was in need of some changes, even though I had no clue where to start. So we planned to invest our income tax return money in buying a house. Unfortunately, when the money came, it was not even half of what we needed to buy the house. I felt so upset, I was even nauseous. Despite the last five years of struggling, all the plans, the momentum, and my goals had completely evaporated — just like that!

My job was not going well; my apartment, my neighbors, my kids, my marriage —everything seemed to be on the verge of destruction. Out of boredom (and probably a sense of self-preservation), I decided to relax and distract myself with a *Lord of the Rings* movie marathon. By the end, I felt totally revived.

I had seen the movies before, yet this time I saw something I had not noticed. I realized that from the very beginning, there was another character in the story. Not one represented by an actor, but by a hidden force, evidenced by the surprising way in which events would turn. A Power which planned for what the

Ring did *not* intend when it deserted Gollum and fell into Bilbo's hands. I saw hope at its best!

At that time, I was reminded of things I'd forgotten. I remembered there would be another day and another opportunity. I looked back in my life and recalled times when I felt drowned by circumstance, yet eventually it all worked out — not just fine, but even better than I had hoped.

Finally, I heard Sam's words as Frodo hung on by his fingertips at the Cracks of Doom. "Don't you let go..." The words seemed meant for *me* at that very time and moment. I hung on tight to hope. I awoke from a sad lethargy of depression and despair. The weight of my world lightened on my shoulders and I breathed easier.

It seems almost strange that a work of fiction, fantasy fiction at that, could have the power to change someone's life. Yet it did. It reminded me to hold on, not to let go, and to hope once again.

Biography: D. Rivera. "I was born in San Juan, PR in1978. After graduating high school and finishing one year at the University of Puerto Rico, I relocated to Arlington, Texas, and three years later to Tampa, Florida, where I met my husband. After the birth of our first daughter, we moved to Millville, New Jersey, where I gave birth to my second child and where we now live. Since I love literature, I hope to complete my Education degree with a major in English and a minor in Spanish."

Lembas for the Soul

Soul-Bound Friendships
Kari Holman

For many reasons, the year *The Fellowship of the Ring* entered theaters will always be a unique one in my life. However, it was the role the movie played in the discovery of my deepest friendship that will forever leave me in its debt.

I was in my last year of high school and was the president of the Science Fiction and Fantasy Club. Many new members joined the club that year, and it was difficult getting to know them all. Somehow, I had completely overlooked the petite, quiet girl who often sat in the middle of everything, until the day we saw *The Fellowship of the Ring*.

The club went to the first showing after school. As president, I positioned myself in the lobby to make sure everyone got to the theater and found where the club was sitting. By the time I was able to take a seat, the only one left was next to the quiet girl whose name I remembered was Patricia. I sized this girl up, thinking, "Geez, she's so small I could break her over my knee!" But when the hobbits were threatened by the Ringwraiths on Weathertop, I found out what a strong handgrip she had!

Even though we had read the book, each new turn and twist delighted us, as if this was our first journey into Middle-earth. Despite my foreknowledge, when Gandalf fell in Moria, I cried. My tough-girl image totally sabotaged by the tears I was shedding, I was taken by surprise when Patricia laid my head in her lap. She gently stroked my hair until I could regain my composure, offering her napkin to use in drying my face. Despite my conviction that I didn't need comforting, I accepted it without question, as I hadn't done since I was a small child. Something

87

Lembas for the Soul

passed between us that night, although we didn't realize it right away. I didn't hear from Patricia again until I got a phone call some weeks later inviting me to go with her family to Chicago for a German festival. I really didn't want to go, but couldn't think of an excuse fast enough. The idea of being roped into spending an evening with a girl I didn't know that well — and her family — had put me in a sour mood by the time Patricia came to the door. But as soon as we started talking, I remembered the three hours we had shared in our tiny movie seats. However, we didn't pick up this new relationship where it had left off. It seemed to spring from nowhere, from a past neither of us had known before. An easiness settled between us, making us feel as though we had known each other for ages.

This reality dawned on me as I started seeing Patricia around school, and we became actual friends. I realized every time I saw Patricia, my world lightened. Everything gave way to a private world between us — even if it only lasted for a few moments. With incredible uneasiness, I broached this idea one day while driving Patricia home from school.

Despite my fears, she didn't freak out. She simply nodded and said, "I've noticed it too. It really feels like we know each other from somewhere. Like our souls have met before." When she spoke those words, our eyes met and unexpectedly, whole lives passed between us. The cards had been laid on the table, and once it had been said, we both realized what we had already sensed. Somehow, in some way, we were bound together in the deepest, most profound sense. If I looked inward, I could feel that interweaving of identities.

There was no way to prove what we felt, just as there is no way to prove when one is in love. You simply know it and there is no need to prove it to anyone. And so it was with Patricia and me. We quietly nurtured our bond and let other people do and think as they would.

Over the next three years, the relationship blossomed into an intimate and nurturing friendship of the deepest kind. There were no secrets kept between us, and nothing could undo the

88

trust and love that had inexplicably formed between us. Most importantly, there was nothing left unsaid between us. We aired out our quarrels and easily forgave, and every day that passed, we found some way to express our love for each other.

Some people call me a hopeless romantic, and I admit this is true. There are some things you must believe in beyond all reason — true love, the powers above, and soul-bound friends are some of the best ones I have found. I consider myself one of the most fortunate people in the world to have found one of my soul-bounded mates.

Even though my dear friend left this world far too early, and I will never again see her beloved face in the sunlight, I can hear her murmuring on the edge of my dreams. "Don't be sad. I've taken the Grey Ships and am happy. When it is your time, you'll take them, too, and we'll meet again on White Shores." It will mean a long time of waiting, but I am prepared to wait. And a friend, be she ordinary or soul-bound, is always worth the wait.

Biography: Kari Holman. Kari is an aspiring fantasy writer finishing her university career at Ohio University in Athens, OH. She has an abundant thirst for travel and enjoys experiencing new cultures and having adventures, as much as she does writing about them. Her three preferred pastimes are medieval re-enactment, writing, and devising new antics to commit with and on her friends. Tolkien has had an immense influence on her life by opening the window to ancient epics and a new brand of storytelling, as well as opening the door to meeting her now inseparable friends.

Lembas for the Soul

Blinded by Shadow

Donna M. Stewart, M.S.

I ring the bell of truth
Of Nature
Of hunger
The ring echoes

I know the sound of innocence
Newest flight of no return
The blue bright ring of sorrow
Never to sing me home

∅

I'm from California, but I know Middle-earth.

I know those fields.

The battle for my Middle-earth began when my sister Marlene became ill with a terminal disease. She was 45.

My brother, Mathew, and I had always been close. Gearing up for our own epic battle brought us closer. We formed a Fellowship of Two to fight for the ones we loved. We battled our fear and pain and fought the process of caring for our terminally ill sister. We fought hard. My brother was my guide and protector, my Strider, and I was his.

Twenty-two months after Marlene died of ALS, my beloved brother and best friend died suddenly and unexpectedly of aortic dissection. Mathew was only 41.

I've thought a lot about why I love *The Lord of the Rings* trilogy, what the stories mean to me, and why I turn to them when I am feeling lonely, sad, or burdened. I love them because I have walked where Frodo walked; I have felt the pain and fear that comes from being thrust into the unknown. I have lived it. I understand the burden of that Ring. I had a ring of my own. I have also returned home to find I have changed and cannot go back. Some hurts do go too deep.

Lembas For the Soul

My sister first introduced me to *The Lord of the Rings* when she was only 14. Marlene read and reread the book throughout her adolescence. I had no interest in the book, because I was an active kid and had no time for books. I was intrigued, but not really interested. But she was. She also owned the three Hildebrandt calendars and displayed them long after they were outdated. I remember those calendars. And I remember her closing the book when she was done, only to pick it up the next day and take the journey again. I was amazed by her ability to read what looked to me like a doorstop made of paper.

Mathew knew of the book and had also watched our sister devour it when he was a little kid. He tried to read the book after our sister died, as a way to remember her, but he could not do it. It was too painful, the journey too long. We decided to wait for the films instead. He and I were looking forward to them, because the book had a long-established presence in our childhood home. We knew we had to see them to honor our sister's memory and to seek solace in something Marlene had held close to her heart for many years. But like the twists in Tolkien's novel, our own journey could not be easily predicted. Mathew died in the summer of 2002, never having seen the first *Rings* movie.

I missed the opening months of *The Fellowship of the Ring* and did not see it until days before it closed at our local theater. I barely remember the movie. I cried through the entire showing. As I sit here now, in June of 2005, I have my keyboard on my lap and a box of tissues at my elbow. The books, the movies, the characters, the metaphors, the emotions, all are fixtures in my life now. The ring of sorrow never sings me home.

I now go to the films to find the love and warmth I had with my family. I find strength from the stories and images. I have fought the battles and understand the metaphors and emotions. I understand the evil that threatens to take away all that we hold dear on this good earth. I've been there. I understand the dark unknown that an evil force can bring. The evil force I faced was illness and death. But evil is evil, whether in the shape of an eye circled in flame, or in the form of an illness that bends and withers a woman to death.

I cry every time I watch *The Return of the King*. Sometimes, I can get to the end of the movie before I cry, but very often I begin to cry when I see Frodo on the volcano with Sam. The image of Sam carrying Frodo is familiar; my brother carried me and I carried him, and together we carried our sister. The image of Frodo's hand as it reaches hard for a handhold and comes away with only rocks and sharp edges makes me cry every time. I have reached for a handhold and come away with only sharp edges, too. Frodo is metaphorically alone, hungry, dehydrated, and knows he will never be the same. I know that feeling. I know the desolation and isolation brought on by a burden no one else understands. I understand. I remember. I was there.

I now watch the trilogy as often as I can. I find a lot of comfort in knowing the burden my brother and I faced, the burden that killed him and that I now carry alone, is universal. Mathew and I joined together to form a Fellowship. We endured the strain of fulfilling a higher purpose. We gave up personal need for the needs of our sister and her son, and for each other. And like *The Fellowship of the Ring*, we did not request a "thank you." We did not need one.

I watch the movies and feel strengthened by them. I realize they are characters in a movie, but that does not matter to me. The feelings, the truths, the pain the characters endured for the good of the ones they love, I understand. I know those battles. I know those fields.

Biography: Donna M. Stewart, M.S. "I am 50 years old and live in Fremont, CA, with my nephew. I hold an M.S. in counseling and human development and enjoy poetry, movies, exercise, and chocolate. I work as an administrative assistant and spend my fun time either in the water, near the water, or wishing I was at the beach. I have lived in the Bay area of California for about ten years and enjoy the closeness of my extended family. I am a free spirit and plan to stay that way."

Lembas for the Soul

The Three Hunters

The Three Hunters

93

The Fellowship of Ringers

Sister Cities
Kathryn Stine

Until *The Lord of the Rings* introduced me to a world of fans and friends, I never knew I had a sister.

I knew of Tolkien's story and the basic plot, but I never had a desire to read the books. Looking back on it now, I guess it wasn't time for me to take the journey. In July 2001, while perusing a bookstore, I saw a one-volume edition of *The Lord of the Rings*. On a life-changing whim, I decided to buy it. Ten days later, I finished the story with tears dripping down my cheeks. How could I have gone 16 years without experiencing this? More importantly, was the experience over now that I had turned the last page?

To my delight, I found my journey was far from finished. I turned to the internet to learn more about Tolkien, his writings and the movies I had heard about. A friend sent me a link to a Tolkien website with a movie photo gallery. After scouring the gallery, I continued exploring the site and found its message board. I told myself I wasn't going to join and, moreover, I wasn't going to become addicted if I did join. Two weeks later, Lady of Rohan had more than 100 posts. Clearly, the One Ring had overcome my resolve.

Over the next two years, the other members and I waited for the movies to be released, argued about what Peter Jackson had done right and wrong, speculated on what the next films would contain, and listed items we wanted to raid from the prop department.

During these discussions, I became friends with a user called Rodia who hailed from Poland. She was a student at film school, close to my age, and called her online persona a hobbit. We were the clichéd "dynamic duo," causing hilarity and chaos wherever we posted. It was always interesting when "Ro" and "Lady Ro" were online.

As 2003 dawned and every day led toward the premiere of *The Return of the King*, our thoughts also turned toward *The Gathering of the Fellowship* in Toronto that December. I was beginning my freshman year of college that fall, and by a cruel twist of fate, final exams fell on the same week as *The Gathering*. It was going to be a great event and I would be stuck in humdrum Indiana, sitting through exams.

Rodia told me she was going to *The Gathering* and suggested I go, too, so we could meet and cause real-life hilarity. I told her my predicament, and she lamented it as well. Then, one of us said, "Is there anywhere else we could meet?"

After extensive research, we decided the best time and place would be Windsor, Ontario, Canada, on December 13, two days before *The Gathering* and the first of my final exams. It was an insane plan, a one-day extravaganza. A mutual friend, Cemthinae, and I left at five a.m., drove to Detroit and crossed the border at Windsor mid-morning.

Everything went according to plan, a few wrong turns aside. Cemthinae and I arrived a few minutes early at the train station. Soon we heard a train's whistle. As people climbed out of the cars, we searched each face. Then we spotted her: a slender figure with a green knit cap and a brown rucksack slung over one shoulder. I smiled. "There's our hobbit!"

A moment later, she gave me a bear hug and enthusiastic greeting. "You're real," she squealed. "You're really *real*!"

"Of course I am." I laughed. "You thought I was CGI?"

We were soon on our way to lunch at a Tim Horton's. At first, conversation was a bit awkward, but it didn't take long for us to become comfortable. We exchanged gifts, including Oreo cookies, which aren't available in Poland but are one of Rodia's favorite snacks. We spent the day wandering around town, talking, laughing, taking pictures, and eventually ending up at the same Tim Horton's for an afternoon snack. This time we were quiet, because we knew our time was getting short.

Finally, we knew it was time to return to the train station. We took a few more pictures, promised to write up accounts of the day, exchanged postal addresses and said goodbye. My last glimpse of Rodia was of her waving from the train window, an Oreo cookie in her hand.

Shortly after the New Year, I found a Hallmark card that read, "If I were a city, you would be my sister city," and mailed it off to her. What made the card so ironic was that she was from Warsaw, Poland, and I was from Warsaw, Indiana. A week later, Rodia sent me an email saying, "You're right. We *are* sisters!"

Since then, we've done many things that sisters do. We have laughed together, told each other secrets, played jokes and gotten angry at each other. The difference is that the Atlantic Ocean is between us. What we can't do over instant messenger, we send through the postal service.

We've exchanged hand-drawn maps of our personal cities, which include places like Oreo cookie factories, MSN Messenger Street, The Shire and other inside jokes. A steady stream of American Oreo cookies and Polish chocolates continues to crisscross the ocean. Even as I write this, my cell phone lights up: a text message from Poland.

Online, we continue to cause chaos and hilarity, although not as often as we used to (college and film school keep us busy). However, we always manage to find time to check up on our sister city and make sure she's doing well and not getting into too much trouble.

Other people may have come away from *The Lord of the Rings* with a deeper understanding of Tolkien's writings or a cool movie souvenir, but I found a sister and best friend. Cheers, Rodia!

Biography: Kathryn Stine. Kathryn (known online as "Lady_of_Rohan" or "SWF ISO Faramir") is a third-year, professional writing major at Taylor University Fort Wayne. As her screen names suggest, her favorite characters are Faramir and Éowyn. She plans to cause chaos and hilarity with Rodia when the latter comes to the United States or the next *Gathering of the Fellowship*.

The Fellowship of the Ring
Joseph Conley

I hear complaints nowadays about the coldness of human contact. Hundreds of people march past each other every day, looking stonily away, feasting their eyes on display windows, magazines, anywhere except back into the eyes of another human being. Actually conversing with someone face to face has become a thing of the past: we talk on cell phones, use the ATM, surf the web, use chat rooms instead of talking to the neighbor. People say there is no community. And yet....

On 9/11, the single most tragic day of my life, I saw images that will remain with me forever. I saw policemen walking into burning buildings without gas masks in the hope of helping someone out alive. I saw lunchrooms and restaurants opening up and giving away free food to those who needed it. I saw people opening up their homes for others to stay in. I saw people come together in what seems to be the coldest and most impersonal place of all, New York City. For a while, just a while, there was community. We didn't care that we had never seen these people before. We didn't care that we were strangers. Just being alive and being with another human being was comforting.

Then the feeling faded, as need and necessity faded. As we forgot what it felt like to be horrified, we forgot what it felt like to be friends with those we didn't know. Does it really take a tragedy to bring out the best in people? We cannot be at our best when we are at our best? It appeared the answer was *yes*. America became divided. Whatever feelings of community and fellowship I felt had faded away, only to resurface with my family at Thanksgiving, when our relatives gathered together. As we held hands and thanked God for what we had before us, I felt at peace within a circle of friends. But then it ended, and I went out into the world. People stared past me and looked at their shoes; when they smiled and gave me my groceries, the smile was forced. My family loves me and that creates community, but the greatest community of all, the community that is shared simply by the connection of being human, is gone, only to reappear at times.

Like this one...

On December 17th, 2003, I tucked my tunic beneath my belt and lifted the green cloak and hood from my bed. My sisters are dressed in their costumes; it's eight-thirty and time to drive to the mall. The line party is supposed to start at nine o'clock, and we haven't left yet.

Arriving we find no line party, and the leader does not show up. We wait in line with a group of other people who think that the line party we were waiting for is also the line party they were waiting for. The line stretches out behind us, people talking and laughing. Some have been waiting for hours, but are still cheerful.

As we resign ourselves to being without the scheduled party, the conversation strikes up among the people standing there. I recognize no faces. No one is familiar, not a single person I have seen before in my life. Some are wearing *Lord of the Rings* costumes and some are not, but they are all wearing smiles. We talk about *The Lord of the Rings*, about the movies and the books, and what we hope and what we fear. Someone has brought the trivia cards and we answer the questions, shouting the answers out above the noise. As the crowd grows, the conversation is harder to hear. Our topic changes to our costumes: how did we make them and how difficult was it? We talk about costume choices and how we wish we had the money to buy the real steel replica swords. Christmas is in eight days and maybe, just maybe....

The conversation drifts from *The Lord of the Rings* to life, and we talk about our families, who was a fan, when we first read the books, and our experiences through life. We laugh a little, make jokes and poke fun at silly animated versions.

I look around and feel at ease among these people I hardly know, who I have met just hours before and hours from now will probably never see again. These people are not strangers to me, but friends, when on any other day we would stare past each other and brush by with a curt "Excuse me" if we feel in the mood. But here, now, on this night, we have stood in line for hours and will stand in line for an hour yet — there is a sense of it in the air. *Community*. We are the Fellowship. Brought together for no reason, as fate and chance might have it, in the right place at the right time, and because of it, on this night, we are friends. For a little while, there is no fear, no hate, no anger, and I know that it will not last. Tomorrow will be a different day, a cold day, but for a little while we are friends. Someday it will come again, the time when we all know each other and we are not afraid to smile. And in between, we will feel empty, because a part of us is missing.

But today, on this night, at this time, we are friends.

For a little while.

Biography: Joseph Conley. "I have been writing short stories, essays, and novels for about six years now. I have written about ten that I have completed, with many more 'on the way'. I just recently I finished a science fiction/comedy novel that, after editing is finished, I hope to have published.

I very rarely write things just for the sake of the story. Usually, I try to include some sort of deeper meaning, not to make the reader agree with me, but simply to raise an issue and make the reader *think* about it. And that, of course, is the basis for this story."

Smote by an Elf Bolt
Louise Newsham

When I was first dragged to the cinema to see *The Fellowship of the Ring*, I had no idea it was going to change my life forever. I know it sounds crazy, but before seeing it, I had nothing much to live for. After the film finished, I just sat there in stunned silence. It deeply touched a part of me I didn't know existed. The courage of The Fellowship inspired me. I vowed to myself to be exactly like them in their loyalty and determination to succeed, even when all hope is lost. Then, maybe someday, I would have close friends like that. And now here I am, three years later, with an Elf of my own, the best friend I could ever ask for.

Before the film, I had never even spoken to her. I felt intimidated by her because she was exactly what I wanted to be: popular, confident and clever. One day, we were both in Spanish class and I saw she had a picture of Legolas in her diary. I couldn't help myself; I blurted out, "You like *The Lord of the Rings*?"

She turned to me and half-shrieked, "*Do I?*" and we immediately hit it off. It's all we ever talked about for the next three years! The moment I first spoke to Sophie, I knew she would be my friend for life and she would stick by me no matter what. She's been through a lot and I'd like to think I've always been there for her.

I am writing this for Sophie — I want to show her just how much I love her and how much she means to me. I've told her I'll stick by her forever. I would go with her to the ends of the earth, just like Sam, because that's how much she means to me. If *The Lord of the Rings* had never been made, I would have missed out on the best thing that ever happened to me. Frodo and Sam's relationship is also truly inspiring. At times I am her Frodo. She looks after me, seeing to it that I eat properly. Then there are times I am *her* Sam, making sure she's safe, and cheering her up when all else fails. She is more than a friend; she is my sister.

"I'm glad to be with you, Sam, here at the end of all things."

If there was ever anyone I would want to be with, the last face I'd see, it would be hers. Because the smile on her face would tell me everything would be all right.

I've only known Sophie for three short years now. Sam and Frodo's bond was forged by amazing events and it held fast until the very end. I know Sophie and I will always be friends. I call her my Elf and I'm her little hobbit. Some things may change, but deep down inside my soul, I know that never will.

Biography: Louise Newsham. "I live in Manchester, England. Although I am still in school, one day I would love to be a film director. Peter Jackson has truly inspired me! I would just like to say to all those reading this: *The Lord of the Rings* is the best book and film ever created. And hello to all my friends — you know who you are, but especially my best mates ever, Nicola and Sophie."

Lord of the What?

Jillian Smith

"The Lord of the *what*? Sorry?" I asked my grade seven teacher.

"*The Lord of the Rings*," he answered patiently. He sounded slightly amused by my question. "We're watching the first movie, *The Fellowship of the Ring*."

"Oh...ok," I replied, and I went to take a seat between my good friends, Elizabeth and Erin. They were chatting about their favourite scenes from the movie. I sat down and listened curiously. "*Frodo*? Is that a kind of bird?" I wondered aloud. "*Mordor*? *Hobbits*?" This movie was going to be interesting; there was no doubt about that.

The movie began and I sincerely enjoyed it, but I admit I didn't understand most of it. Elizabeth and Erin both whispered explanations to me, giving me a play-by-play of every scene. Well, that was two and a half years ago, and let's just say, things have changed a lot! Having seen *The Fellowship of the Ring* 49 times since then, I can safely say I don't need a play-by-play anymore. I've also seen the other two movies almost as many times.

The Lord of the Rings has enriched my life so profoundly that I decided to become a member of the Official Fan Club. Not only have the movies and books inspired me, but Howard Shore's beautiful and powerful songs have motivated me to write music of my own on the piano. I entered one of my creations in a composition competition and I won first place! That is just one small, yet not insignificant, effect that *The Lord of the Rings* has had on my life.

Lembas For the Soul

Because of these films, I have rekindled old friendships with people with whom I had lost touch. The movies also motivated me to learn how to speak Elvish. These influential and life-changing movies have made me a better person. I am more positive and optimistic. I have more hope and confidence in everything I do.

At my soccer game last week, we played an undefeated team. Some of my teammates were depressed and they thought the game was over before it even started. I did not lose hope. Even though we still lost that game (2-1), I ended up scoring on a breakaway!

Overall, these beautiful books and movies have enriched my life. They have lifted a veil and changed the way I view nature. The flowers simply look more colourful and the trees look more youthful. The wind makes music in the tree boughs.

This emotional and powerful story taught me so many lessons I will keep for the rest of my life. It helped me build stronger friendships and showed me the importance of love and fellowship, and that everything happens for a reason.

These masterpieces — the books and the movies — have taught me the importance of sacrifice. Without sacrifice, you gain nothing of importance. *The Lord of the Rings* is unique in its vision and historical depth. J.R.R. Tolkien has touched my heart, given me hope and made me believe in my dreams. Now it's time for him to do the same for you.

Biography: Jillian Smith. "My name is Jillian Rene Smith. I'm 15 years old and I live in in a small town in Ontario, Canada, about 45 minutes from Niagara Falls. My parents' names' are Jim and Kim and I also have two sisters, Nicole and Kaylie, and a brother, Michael.

I love playing sports, including soccer, basketball, volleyball, baseball, swimming and track. I enjoy reading, writing, watching movies, hanging out with my friends, and I love music. I've been playing the piano for nine years; I can play the guitar, drums, harmonica and the French horn."

A Turn in the Path

Krista Messer

A few years ago, I saw a trailer for *The Fellowship of the Ring*. I had never heard of *The Lord of the Rings* and dismissed the movie, thinking it was just another lame fantasy. A few years later, my brother got *The Fellowship of the Ring* and *The Two Towers* on DVD. At first I was reluctant to watch them, but then I figured it couldn't hurt. So one night, we sat down and watched them back-to-back. As soon as *The Two Towers* ended, I was very glad I'd given *LOTR* a chance.

I found it difficult to wait the next few months for the release of *The Return of the King* in the theater. The day I saw that movie was the day it became official — I was, and still am, in love with everything Middle-earth-related. Since then, I've made my mom run out and get me all the Tolkien books I've ever heard of. I read all of *The Lord of the Rings*, then *Unfinished Tales, The Silmarillion* and others. I've become completely captivated by everything Tolkien.

All of my life I've been a shy person. Talking to people just isn't something I can easily do. That had never been a big problem until I started high school, about the same time I fell in love with *LOTR*. Eventually, I realized my "obsession" with *LOTR* was really bugging my mom. She told me she wished I wouldn't like *LOTR* so much because it was doing nothing productive for me and would ultimately to lead to social issues. That made me decide to work on my shyness problem.

To battle my bashful qualities, I auditioned for a school play. We had to perform a monologue for the director. Since I always wanted to tie important events in my life to *LOTR*, I performed

Lembas for the Soul

Galadriel's opening monologue to *The Fellowship of the Ring*. Unfortunately, I didn't get a role, but I didn't let that discourage me. I kept practicing and auditioned again for the school's musical the next semester. This time, I made it!

Over the next two months I made many new friends. I have become very close to a few of my fellow cast members who are interested in *LOTR* and anything else concerning Middle-earth. Our shared *LOTR* obsession made it easier to get to know each other because that's all we talked about for the first few weeks. My new friends have also introduced me to their friends. I used to never let anyone introduce me, but now I will gladly meet new people.

I used to avoid talking to anybody, even if I had something I really wanted to share. Once I became more confident, I realized that people liked it when I spoke up. So I began piping up when people mentioned something I knew a lot about. I used *LOTR* as a sort of stepping-stone to help me along the way. Now I'll even say goodbye to people with *"Namárië,"* which is something I had avoided using with someone who wasn't a *LOTR* fan.

The Lord of the Rings has really helped me make new friends and become less shy. I'm not half as afraid of life as I used to be. For that, I thank Eru every day.

Biography: Krista Messer. "My name is Krista, but I'm also widely known as Elle, which is short for Ellehcim, my online alias. I love acting, singing, and spending lots of time posting on a few online *LOTR* message boards. My absolute favorite message board is nicknamed *TORC* (TheOneRing.com), and I owe most of my knowledge of Middle-earth to the people there. In fact, I spend so much time there you'd never know I'm as active as I am! But mostly, I'm a unique 16-year-old girl who loves to hang out with her best friends, Ashley, Brittany, and Sara."

My Journey to Rivendell
Éireen

Whenever I look back to when I first heard about *The Lord of the Rings,* it always brings a smile to my face. I can still remember that moment as clearly as if it was today. My brother told me he had a DVD of the first part of the trilogy, *The Fellowship of the Ring*, and my entire family decided to watch it. After the first half hour of the movie, I quit watching it, deciding it was the worst movie I had ever seen. I pushed any thought of *The Lord of the Rings* out of my head, and forgot about it altogether. I had never been interested in fantasy fiction, anyway.

Then a few months later, my brother told me he was about to watch *Fellowship* again. Since I was totally bored, I decided to watch it once again, hoping I would be able to watch it all the way through. This time, not only did I manage to watch the movie until the end, but I got so caught up in the story I could not forget about it. When I found out it would be two more years until I could see how the story ended, I started to panic. The next day, I bought *The Lord of the Rings* in print and spent the next few days reading it, almost without any breaks. I fell in love with the books and I began to discover Tolkien's magical world.

By coincidence, I found *The Council of Elrond (www.councilofelrond.com)* which is one of the best Tolkien websites on the internet. I started to learn Elvish, using the *Sindarin* course on that site. I loved the beautiful language of the Elves. Without paying attention to the comments of people around me, who were sure I had to be crazy, I devoted much time to learning it. It is still one of my favorite pastimes.

Lembas for the Soul

Then, last summer I discovered the thing that became my biggest hobby and also allowed me to meet many amazing people. I was on *The Council of Elrond* site and came across the RPG (Role Playing Game) part of the site. I had never been in that section, probably because I had no idea what RPG really meant. Since I had a lot of time, I decided to see what it was. I read a couple of RPG threads, and decided to join them and have a go at role-playing. And that was one of the best decisions I ever made.

Why? There is no one answer to this question. I have been role-playing for almost one year now, and it has never bored me. Thanks to role-playing in the world created by Tolkien, I have made many wonderful friends from all over the world, and a few very close friends I meet every day on the internet. This is really special to me, to be able to meet with great people who share my interests and with whom I can talk for hours and hours without getting bored.

Thanks to role-playing and my friends, I discovered my passion for writing. I had never been interested in writing, and if someone had told me a year ago that I would be creating my own stories, I would have never believed them. Now, I write stories that are hundreds of pages long, sometimes by myself, and other times collaborating with my friends. And I love doing it.

After thinking about it, I guess that it is also my main reason for writing this story. I want to share my joy with all of you who are reading this. I am very happy to have discovered Tolkien's wonderful books, and to have found out how pleasant and rewarding it is to write something of my own. I also wanted to thank all my amazing friends for being with me all the time, through good — and also some difficult — moments. You make my days bright, and I really cannot imagine my life without you, my friends. I hope we will never decide to part our ways. I also am sure I will never stop loving Tolkien's books, because I will always remember what they have brought to me, and how they have changed my life for better, and made it more interesting ... for good.

Lembas For the Soul

Dedicated to my two dearest *mellyn*, Nar and Vana. Thank you for everything. I love you so much! Never forget about it.
—Éireen.
And here, last but not least, I would also like to thank my family. I love you all very much.
—Iza

Biography: Éireen. "My real name is Izabela Karnas, though all my friends know me as Éireen. I am a young woman living in Poland, and am currently a student. My free time is filled mostly with Live Role Playing and writing. If you'd like to find out something more about me, or just feel like writing to me, then feel free to. My email address is sidhpeace@gmail.com."

For Gandalf

Brenda DeBord Tuttle

Those of us who love the works of J.R.R. Tolkien, especially *The Lord of the Rings*, are proudly called Ringers. How appropriate, since during a difficult time in my life I felt like a "ring of friendship and mutuality" surrounded me.

When I first met my husband some 26 years ago, Steven asked me if I had read *The Lord of the Rings*. I had not, probably because fantasy was not part of my reading life. My soon-to-be husband, a very great fan, insisted I read the book. How glad and thankful I am; I fell in love with Middle-earth, all its characters, and the entire realm of valor, integrity, love, honesty, bravery and humor. Steven called himself Gandalf; for myself I chose the name *Eledhwyn* — Elf sheen.

Eventually, we had two sons, and as a family we read *The Hobbit* and *The Lord of the Rings*. My husband and I also went on to read *The Silmarillion*. When we visited England, we imagined the hedge-lined roads we rode upon or walked along were in The Shire.

Some years later, Steven was killed in a plane crash on September 22, Bilbo's and Frodo's birthday. I had lost my wonderful husband, lover, best friend and father to my children. Although I was blessed with a fantastic support group in my family, friends and church members, the loneliness and emptiness still weighed heavy on my heart.

Then one day, as I skimmed the internet, I saw *The Lord of the Rings* was being made into a feature-length, live-action movie. I became quite interested to see how this was going to be

109

accomplished and which actors would play the various characters. I was worried the films would not reflect Tolkien's values, nor his brilliant, flowing language. To me, the narrative and dialogue in the book were like music without the notes.

I came across a variety of websites about the movie and the book and spent much time exploring them. I enjoyed "meeting" other people who were as passionate about Middle-earth as I was. When I discovered the extended work done on Tolkien's Elvish languages, I was both fascinated and excited. Steven and I had shared a love of different languages.

Over the next few years, as more information about Tolkien's works, languages and the film adaptation became available, I had a new focus, activities which kept me going during the lonely hours in the evening. I found a sense of companionship with others who were also waiting for the movies to unfold. In a sense, I was sharing it with my husband, who would have loved to be a part of this excitement and see his favorite book come to life.

I think one of the greatest gifts J.R.R. Tolkien gave the world is the reminder that virtues are not things of the past — that they are still of great worth and should be embraced. By so carefully and lovingly crafting his movies to reflect Tolkien's vision, Peter Jackson has kept those same virtues alive and exposed a whole new generation to those noble ideals.

In the films' enthusiastic worldwide reception, we've seen how modern society *hungers* for great literature, something that shows us we can aspire to be something better than ourselves. In a media world sodden with profanity, vulgarity and mindless violence, *The Lord of the Rings* shines all the brighter. The book and the movies have brought families together in their shared love of the story, and have also encouraged people to read and search out more literature like it.

Having the movies come to an end is like having a beloved guest leave. But thankfully, the book will always be available so we can open it and revisit Frodo, Gandalf, Aragorn, the Elves, Dwarves and all of Middle-earth. I wouldn't mind settling down in Rivendell myself. As a matter of fact, I think I'll just head that way now....

Biography: Brenda DeBord Tuttle. Brenda currently lives in Crozet, Virginia with her cat, Arwen. She studied voice performance and choral conducting at the University of Alaska Anchorage; has directed church choirs, accompanied a voice class at UAA, taught private voice and piano and has sung in several choral groups. Brenda currently sings with the Oratorio Society of Charlottesville-Albemarle.

Brenda was first introduced to *The Lord of the Rings* by her husband, Steven and immediately fell in love with it. Like her husband, she loves different languages and speaks German, a little Dutch and Welsh. She is particularly fascinated by the Elvish languages.

Pippin's Dream

Welcome to the Hall of Fire

The Dragon Seeker
Kristina Ricks

I have been hunting for dragons all my life. I grew up with my nose in a book, especially books filled with swords, knights, princesses, and magic. While the other girls read *Teen Magazine*, I read my copy of *The Voyage of the Dawn Treader* by C.S. Lewis until the pages fell out. I was Lucy Pevensie, I was Frodo, I was Sparrowhawk. When I met my husband years later, what clinched the deal for me was not our mutual interest in backpacking, travel, or bicycling, nor that he made me laugh, but that he knew his *Nazgul* from his *Uruk-Hai*.

I approached Peter Jackson's movies with trepidation. How could any film capture the Middle-earth of my imagination? But Jackson swept me into his version of the story with *The Fellowship of the Ring*, despite his sometimes maddening departures from the text. The black riders, the tower of Orthanc, Ian McKellen's Gandalf, the pure visual spectacle had me hooked. I eagerly awaited the next installments.

In August 2002, I bought the DVD of *Fellowship*. While the movie was still just as good, it was the interviews that captivated me. I watched every one; not only with the actors, but with the set designers, the animators, the artists, the animal trainers, and the armorers. I would have watched an interview with a sandwich maker if it had been there. These were ordinary people like me, whose shared passion brought this movie to life. Again and again, I was struck by their dedication, their love for Tolkien's world, and their genuine enthusiasm. The thought kept occurring to me: what the hell am I doing with my life? Where am I going?

When I first watched these interviews, my children were two and four. My work as a software technical writer had gone from the frantic, exciting mid-90s at a start-up firm to the company's bankruptcy and my layoff in 2001. I gave my heart and soul to that company, spilled far too much ink and burned a lot of midnight oil, and spent my creativity only to be among the half who didn't keep their jobs when the company filed for bankruptcy.

Where I landed by 2002 was just a job, enough to pay the bills, nice people, but never anything more. I knew better — my fulfillment would never again come from a corporation, no matter how often they told me, "Our employees are like family."

The question lingered. What was I doing? About the same time, I found a copy of Stephen King's *On Writing*. Between that and the *Fellowship* interviews, my dreams from years ago reawakened. I remembered I always wanted to write — real books, not just technical manuals. But that's too scary! What if I'm not any good? But Stephen King kept at me. *Write every day*, he said. *Get to know who your muse is and feed him or her with regular practice. Magic will happen if you do the work.* King has a wonderful, blue-collar, encouraging manner about writing. *You can do this*, he said.

I have discovered the delightful hour of five a.m., with no one awake to say "Mom!" for every crisis. I can't do housework (even if I wanted to) for fear of waking everyone up. My coffee maker has a timer on it, so a steaming pot is ready for me. The dog is up, briefly, before collapsing to snooze beside my chair while I write. In that one hour of the day my brain is fresh, cleared of work, children, bills, and dishes. I live in another world with my own characters, slowly and with many false starts, bringing them to life.

I am trying, of course, to write fantasy, to develop a world of my own like those to which I've always traveled in books. Someone who writes stories set in the real world can think "1928

Iowa chicken farm" and do research at the library or the local historical society to populate it with realistic settings and objects (Model-T Ford, Herbert Hoover, farmhouse, newspapers, letters from Aunt Ida in New York City, kerosene lamps). Fantasy, however, provides no such luxury. I'm on my own. I have to constantly examine my world. Is that idea for how the magic works original, or did I read it once in … oh, dang.

But it's fun not having a ready-made world. I constantly confront problems I haven't thought out yet. How do family relationships work? What does one eat for breakfast? Who was the current king's father and how did he die? What happens at a funeral? Tolkien also imagined these details for his Middle-earth many times for his own entertainment. Yet in spite of my love for all things Elvish, I admit I've never waded through *The Silmarillion*. It is the backstory of *The Lord of the Rings*, and there's a reason it didn't make it into the main book. In some places it has the narrative interest of the begats in the Bible. So while I lovingly construct the history, politics, and a myriad of other information about my fantasy world, I can't lose myself in it. I must still have compelling characters and a good story that moves along, makes internal sense, and pushes a reader to turn the page.

The work is maddeningly slow. I don't know what I'm doing. However, stopping brings back that fundamental question: what am I doing with my life? I've had to take breaks — longer than I would like — because my family always comes before the writing. During this project, my husband has gone from full-time dad at home (and I didn't appreciate how good I had it until it was over!) to full-time nursing student. But I manage to find my way back, to steal an hour here or there. I've taken classes and read books. I apply the same philosophy to my creative writing as I do to my paid employment: educate myself, grow, work hard, and try again. I try to remember that Tolkien took 18 or more years to write *The Lord of the Rings* — all while he worked full-time, raised four children, and graded exam papers for extra money.

Tolkien relied on his like-minded literary friends — C.S. Lewis, Charles Williams, Owen Barfield and others, a group that called themselves The Inklings. They met on Tuesday lunchtimes at The Eagle and Child pub in Oxford. My own critique group also meets, ironically enough, on Tuesday lunchtimes, but in a nondescript, windowless conference room. I've been to The Eagle and Child pub (or "The Bird and Baby" as the Inklings affectionately called it), as a tourist, too many years ago. While the pub is certainly more picturesque than our conference room, I know my group strives toward the same goals as The Inklings. We all struggle with fitting writing into our busy lives. My critique group provides support, encouragement, and above all, honest, thorough editing. I am deeply in their debt, although I'll admit coming away sometimes wanting to cry and kick my filing cabinets. But I know that when I'm "on," they'll tell me that, too. When I've earned it, their praise is real. With the toughness and collective editing pens of Heather, Anita, Jason, and Cindy, I'm a much better writer than I would have been. We share each other's successes — Heather's first novel will be published in October 2005, and the group has edited several drafts of this essay.

A quote from Carl Jung now hangs above my writing desk: "Nothing has a stronger influence psychologically on one's environment and especially on one's children than the unlived life of the parent." Sometimes I write *because* of my children, as well as in spite of them. I want them to understand they can follow their dreams, too, however improbable. Peter Jackson and Fran Walsh, the husband-and-wife team behind *The Lord of the Rings* films, did so while raising two young children amid the chaos of a demanding seven-year project. When my life gets crazy, I think of Peter and Fran. Although I don't have the nannies and staff that they probably do, I share at least some of their chaos. I can survive it.

I'm still working on that novel, and I'm proud to say I finished a first draft. In the spirit of first drafts, it's pretty bad. It needs a good, stiff edit and quite a lot of propping up. But it is on paper. When I lose my way in my writing, I watch those interviews on my now large collection of *Lord of the Rings* DVDs. Those people believed passionately in what they were doing. They worked and worked and worked until they got it right. They followed their dreams, one ring of chain mail at a time. I can do the same.

Biography: Kristina Ricks. Kristina lives in Beaverton, Oregon, with her husband, two children, and a Labrador mutt. She is a mom, a wife, and a writer, although the order of those changes depending on the day. Her novel is in pieces all over the floor as she hacks and slashes it into something that anyone would want to read. Her greatest joy in life is reading *The Hobbit* to her son, who is now seven.

Lembas for the Soul

Lighting the Beacon
Aline E. Doering

Many years ago, in eighth grade, I picked up a copy of *The Hobbit* in the school library. I had been told about this book and how good it was, so I decided to check it out myself. I had been reading fantasy stories for a while, and Tolkien was always highly rated. I should be able to read this book, right? Wrong. No matter how hard I tried, I couldn't read past the first paragraph. A few months later, I tried again with *The Fellowship of the Ring* and encountered the same problem. Looking back now, I think it may have been bad timing or something.

On December 19, 2001, I was just one of the many who went to the opening day showing of *The Lord of the Rings: The Fellowship of the Ring*, the first in a trilogy of movies directed by Peter Jackson. I came away from the theater very much hooked. My friends laughed at me. I was still being stubborn about reading the books, even after seeing the movie. My reasoning was that if I couldn't read the books in school, I wouldn't be able to read them at all. So, I asked questions instead, and was placated only a few times before being told to go read the books. Still, I was stubborn about it, and waited for the second installment to arrive in theaters.

Once again, I found myself in line for *The Two Towers* on opening day. This time, I was with a small group of friends who were just as excited as I was. The only difference? They had read the books. Afterwards, we spent hours in the parking lot, discussing the movie. Each time I asked a question, or speculated as to what the next movie would involve, or mentioned that I thought Aragorn and Eowyn would get married, I was directed to read the books. The discussion would continue on, but since I hadn't read the books, I couldn't follow it.

Months before the opening of *The Return of the King*, I gave in. I went to one of the local bookstores and bought the trilogy. In two weeks, I finished *Fellowship* and *Two Towers*, leaving *The Return of the King* until after the movie. My friends

118

urged me to go ahead and finish the series, but I was being stubborn again. I didn't want to spoil seeing the movie! With another small group of friends, I made the journey to the theater to see the last of the movie trilogy. We spent time in the parking lot, talking about the movies overall and how much we would miss seeing more. I went home, got the last book and simply devoured it. I was done in a matter of hours and then I dove into the appendices.

To this day, I still marvel at how I was able to read the trilogy so quickly, and after that, I read *The Silmarillion* and *Unfinished Tales* in three weeks. Needless to say, I was now an official Tolkien fan, and this led me to look for others via the internet.

It was a cold day, January 19th, 2004, when I joined the *LOTR* discussion group on Yahoo. I was prompted by the need to settle a slight argument. A friend claimed Aragorn and Arwen never married, that Arwen left for the Undying Lands, and Aragorn actually married a Gondorian lady. I had just finished reading the books, so I was confident that Aragorn did marry Arwen, who became the Queen of Gondor, and was mother to his son and heir, Eldarion, along with an unnumbered amount of sisters. My first post to the list was about that argument, and soon I had my answer and knew I had won the argument. I emailed my best friend, gave her the correct passages, and that was the final word.

I can't quite pinpoint the exact moment I was urged to begin writing, but in March of that same year, I was invited to join another list. This one was centered on fanfic, and a group of authors had been writing a story together. It intrigued me enough to want to create a character, build her story, and then see where she fit into the larger story. With the help of one of the authors, who is now one of my best friends, I had my character set for entry into the story. While this sounds a lot like RPG (Role Playing Game), the group claimed that RPG was not what it was about. In any case, I was given the chance to write a few introductory chapters for my character, and then I was in the 'game', as it were.

Several months later, I parted ways with the first fanfic group and found myself joining two more. I have written 16 stories of various lengths, and I am currently writing several more, co-authoring with my best friend, whom I mentioned above. My brand of writing tends to blend a healthy mix of both Tolkien characters and my own. I am proud to say I have also won an online writing contest, earning a digital certificate and having my story placed in the fan fiction section of the site that held the contest. I have my stories posted in several archives online, and my friend and I have a joint website that holds all of our works. I am also currently working on an original fantasy story, non-Tolkien related, and I hope to have it finished and posted by the end of April.

The amazing thing about all of this: I hadn't been able to write anything for 11 years. The last thing I wrote was a short story in high school, and it was part of an English class assignment. Once I graduated, I had lost my motivation to write. I tried a few times, but I would just sit and stare at the paper or the screen, wondering what I wanted to do with the idea in my head that refused to come out. It must have been some kind of unbreakable writer's block, a wall only the *LOTR* movies could breach. For that, I am ever grateful to Peter Jackson, and everyone involved, for bringing the books to life for me. I am grateful to my friends, who were as stubborn as I was when it came to reading the books. Most of all, I am grateful to Professor Tolkien, who had the genius and wherewithal to write his stories in the first place. If he hadn't, I would not be telling my tale.

Biography: Aline E. Doering. Aline lives in southeast Tennessee with her monster Italian Greyhound and six mackerel tabbies. She's worked for the local CBS affiliate for nearly nine years as an editor. If the opportunity arises, she'd like to try her hand at editing for movies. Away from work, she contents herself with her writing and devoting time to her friends and family.

Lembas for the Soul

From Bag End to the Darkling Woods
Catharine Mallard

In January 2002, I sat in a darkened theater with my husband as *The Fellowship of the Ring* came on the screen. Cate Blanchett's voice cast a spell of enchantment and my own adventure began. I had never heard of a hobbit, or read the works of J.R.R. Tolkien; but here was this place in my heart, a place that just seemed to be waiting for them. When the film was over, I headed straight to the bookstore and dove into the writings of Tolkien, reading *LOTR*, *The Hobbit*, *The Letters* and biographies. I was on the fast track to geekhood.

All seemed normal after that, with Middle-earth tucked safely in that place where beloved tales live, and I waited for the DVD release of *The Fellowship of the Ring*.

Very soon, quiet inspiration translated into some fairly unusual, even daring actions. I was swept away by Arwen's chase scene in the theater, and a childhood dream was rekindled. After reading about Eowyn and the Rohirrim, I decided to take riding lessons as a bit of adventure. As Frodo says in Rivendell, "My own adventure turned out quite different." My lessons ended with me being rushed by ambulance to the nearest emergency room. I took a bad spill when the 17-hand dressage horse I was riding took off at full canter. I broke my right arm in two places and suffered extensive nerve damage. The doctors surgically reconstructed my arm, and uncertainty prevailed on the degree of damage that could be permanent.

To lose use of my dominant hand and arm was terrifying. My identity as an artist and teacher was shaken. Even my home life as wife and mother wasn't the same. I was forced to sit on the sidelines while friends and family took my daughters school shopping, and I attempted to scrawl lesson plans with my left hand for my substitute, not knowing when I would be able to return to teaching.

I took comfort in re-reading *LOTR*, started researching Tolkien online and came across the *theOneRing.net* (*TORn*) which would become my online home. I joined in the discussions, learning from Tolkien scholars and sharing stories with other "newbies". And as if all this wasn't gift enough, something magical started to happen. As I experienced fans' poems, stories and art online, my own artistic direction changed.

I had fallen in love with myth and fairy tales as a child and became an admirer of many fairy tale illustrators, then the pre-Raphaelite artists as I grew up. However, illustrative art wasn't encouraged when I was at university, so I went along with the flow, trying to be the kind of artist they were producing, although never really finding my voice.

Then came the long-awaited arrival of *The Fellowship* DVD. The work of Alan Lee in the appendices opened a floodgate, connecting *LOTR* to my lifelong love of mythic art. I was so moved by watching Mr. Lee as he sketched, how his art took on a life of its own as he worked. I'm an art teacher and have taken great joy in inspiring my students on their artistic path, nurturing them as they find their own style and blossom as young artists. But until seeing Alan Lee's work and hearing him describe his process, no one had inspired me in a way that touched my artist's heart. Here was someone showing me the way. The door that had been locked for so long had just swung open.

As I regained use of my hand, I started some small sketches of scenes from Tolkien's work and posted them on *TORn*. Encouraged by the feedback from fellow Tolkien fans on *TORn*, I continued drawing and sharing Tolkien-inspired artwork. One of the most rewarding experiences has been to collaborate with other Tolkien artists and writers. Through *LOTR*, my connections with other fans around the world have led to friendships that I can't imagine my life without. I have illustrated poetry for online writer friends. I have worked with a young film student in Atlanta who has become my web designer. I'm collaborating with a glass artist in France, providing designs for her elvish jewelry.

Lembas for the Soul

I met many of my online friends in person for the first time in 2004 in Atlanta, at the *TORn* Moot for the Howard Shore symphony, and Alan Lee's art exhibit. I'll never forget the excitement of seeing so many online friends in person while waiting to meet Alan Lee. I had written a thank-you letter to Mr. Lee to tell him what an inspiration he was to me. I had placed the letter along with a couple of my prints in a sealed envelope and had given it to his assistant. But my friends wouldn't let that lie. While I'm standing, teary-eyed over meeting him, they tell him my art is in the envelope. He gets the package and opens it right then. There is Alan Lee looking at my paintings, right in front of me. I thought I would fall through the floor! He carefully read the letter and looked — really *looked* — at the painting and proceeded to talk to me about them as he might to any artist. It was a dream come true.

My exposure to Tolkien's work gave me the artistic inspiration and confidence to follow my own inner voice. My most ambitious project to date is collaboration with a fellow Tolkien fan on a series of original stories and illustrations involving nature spirits. I'm enjoying the adventures of being an artist every step of the way.

Biography: Catharine Mallard. Catharine lives in Florida with her husband of 17 years and two daughters. A public school art teacher for 16 years, she received her degree in Art Education from the University of Florida and is a National Board Certified teacher. Her work has been shown throughout the U.S. and in 2005 was displayed at The Tolkien Society's Fiftieth Anniversary of *The Lord of the Rings* Conference in Birmingham, England. Catharine also serves on the Mythic Imagination Institute's Teacher Development Committee. In addition to creating Tolkien-inspired art, Catharine is collaborating with fellow Tolkien fan and writer Dana Sterling on the mythological story cycle, "Winter's Muse". You can visit Catharine's online gallery at www.darklingwoods.com.

A Lord of the Rings Spell

Dana P. Clark

I had never paid much attention to Tolkien's *The Lord of the Rings* until I saw Peter Jackson's film rendition of *The Fellowship of the Ring*. That film was so spiritually uplifting, I have since read the books and vow to read them once a year, the same as actor Christopher Lee. I also continue to watch Peter Jackson's film trilogy masterpiece over and over again. Not only have the special relationships between members of the Fellowship kept me spellbound, but *The Lord of the Rings* is one of only a few stories where I can identify with almost every key character. I grew rather attached to these characters, so at a time of great darkness in my own life, Middle-earth became a refuge for me. My life has never been the same.

The Fellowship meets on the brink of the worst of times for Middle-earth. They come from different ways of life, knowing very little about one another, and in spite of these circumstances, they care about one another. They are true to themselves, and they come together for the common good of everyone. In particular, Sam's loyalty to Frodo, as exhibited in the drowning scene towards the end of *The Fellowship of the Ring*, deeply affected me and made me curious to find out what was to become of them. I envy the friendship between Frodo and Sam, because some of my friendships unfortunately did not withstand the test of time as theirs did.

Aragorn and Boromir's strained relationship also interested me. Boromir doubts Aragorn is Isildur's Heir, and resents that the Company ignores his suggestion to go to Mordor by way of Gondor. Yet at Boromir's death scene, Aragorn honors him, in

124

spite of his attempt to take the Ring from Frodo. Both feel as though they have failed the other members of the Fellowship. That scene speaks volumes of the power of forgiveness and reconciliation, and it also displays the true character of two noble and extraordinary men. I have compassion for Boromir, who had all the good intentions in the world for his people, but never lived to see them through. Nor did he ever fully understand why another road was taken instead of the one he would have chosen for the Company.

In fact, as Boromir learned, there are many things that happen in our world that one can't understand, and never before had I experienced such a frustrating feeling than when I met up with misfortune in my own life. I worked for an architecture firm in an extremely demanding and stressful job. My supervisor was a micro-managing dictator. Things deteriorated when I received an adversarial performance review, which included an ultimatum, demanding that I recommit myself to complete servitude in order to prove myself worthy of remaining employed. He thought the problem was my bad attitude, not that I needed extra help in order to meet the unexpected, increased demands of our client.

So, what was I going to do? To simply quit my job when we had bills to pay might have seemed rather absurd, and under these circumstances, hurt my reputation and future job prospects. But was it worth it to endure more stress, not to mention humiliation, just to prove my supervisor wrong and keep a paycheck? Maybe *The Two Towers* and *The Return of the King* weighed heavily on my mind at this time, but I compared my situation to that of Captain Faramir, who has trouble living up to the unrealistic expectations of his father, Lord Denethor. Denethor blames the defeat at Osgiliath on his perceived notion that Faramir lacks the will to defeat the enemy, rather than face the fact that the men of Gondor were vastly outnumbered.

My supervisor treated me in a similar way, by telling me that I had also failed in spite of my efforts. I then thought of Captain Faramir's other dilemma, when he encounters Frodo and the Ring, and has to decide whether to "show his quality" and deliver the Ring to Lord Denethor, or let Frodo continue on his quest to destroy the ring, even if it meant forfeiting Faramir's future and reputation in Gondor. After remembering Captain Faramir's decision — *it is forfeit* — I made up my mind, and turned in my resignation letter.

So it was that I left my job with my dignity intact, but I was still depressed, exhausted, and unfulfilled. This incident unfortunately left me feeling much less trustworthy of others, for there were evil forces at work all around me. My home and lake house in the woods by the water were peaceful places in which to dwell and shut out the rest of the world. I understood why the Elves of Lothlorien preferred not to venture from their protected, unsullied wood and into the dark and dangerous lands around it.

Still, I felt free and concluded I had not been happy in my career. My past employment had consisted of a lot of "metal and wheels" jobs, which lacked autonomy, interest and creativity. I remember sitting in the office on a beautiful spring day, looking out the window and longing, as Bilbo did, to see mountains again. I also thought of Aragorn, before he returned to the throne of Gondor, so free to wander alone in the wilderness instead of being confined indoors to someone else's service. Considering all of these thoughts, I decided I'd better start thinking about, as Gandalf said, what to do with the time that is given to me.

A "little person" like me can feel insignificant, which is why I feel especially connected to the hobbits. In *The Lord of the Rings*, the least likely of creatures in Middle-earth do alter the course of the future. That has helped me to change my way of thinking and believe in myself again. So it is ironic that through this terrible experience and my newly discovered passion for *The Lord of the Rings*, one of my lifelong dreams resurfaced. I've always wanted to write. I had thought it was too unrealistic an aspiration to pursue, until now. Writing this story is a start. And as I have been researching my options, I am energetic, excited and uplifted again, as never before. Maybe it is a "spell", or simply what someone experiences when they follow their heart.

In addition, I intend to follow my heart "there and back again." Throughout Middle-earth there is evidence of ancient realms and cultures that existed long ago, which, until their journey, many in the Fellowship had only heard about or remembered in song and tales. Before the hobbits set out on their journey to Rivendell, they were content with their quiet, peaceful existence in the Shire. Many people in our world who never travel or become exposed to other cultures probably feel that way. I do not want to lose perspective, being too caught up in the happenings in my small part of our universe. I realize I have sat idle too long and have become restless. I now plan to travel again, including various areas of Tolkien's England and New Zealand.

The key characters in *The Lord of the Rings* have all made an impact on my life, but it was thanks mostly to Captain Faramir that for once, I found the courage to listen to my heart and conscience, not other people's opinions, and walk away from what was a no-win situation. In fact, this was the first time any character in a story influenced me to do anything as drastic as quit a job!

A prominent theme in *The Lord of the Rings* is the value Tolkien places on storytelling. In my view, it is through old songs and tales that profound meaning and truth about life can be found. Tolkien encourages us to recognize that in our own lives, tell the story of our own journey down that road, and pass it on to those who will come after us. Years from now, when we celebrate the 25th anniversary of the release of the Peter Jackson films, we can reflect on seeing them for the first time and remember how they changed our lives. That is why I want to write and travel again: I have my own "there and back again" story waiting to be told.

Biography: Dana P. Clark. Dana (also known as Daelinloth, Hobbit of the Shire) is an aspiring writer who lives with her husband Jake and their "fat hobbit cat", Ewok, in Kansas City, Missouri. She enjoys gardening, cooking, playing music and other creative pursuits, as most hobbits do. She and Jake escape the stifling city environment whenever they can and head to their own "woodland realm" on beautiful Lake of the Ozarks, Missouri.

Set Aglow
Karime Limon-Rico

My second pregnancy was very difficult, not at all like the relatively easy time I had with my first baby. This time around, I ached all over, my feet were swollen, I had terrible heartburn day and night, and I was deeply depressed. I had to quit my job because of the miserable way I was feeling. And this time my husband and I fully realized what a huge responsibility we had, to carefully nurture the two young ones in our care. The weight of that reality was crushing us. Yet despite the pain and worry, it was a momentous experience to have my second baby girl. To see my three-year-old daughter's excitement about being a big sister was a joy in itself.

On Christmas of 2003, I received *The Silmarillion* from my husband. Soon, I found that not being able to sleep because of the new baby was not such a hardship. In fact, I voluntarily stayed awake. The richness of Tolkien's characters and the world surrounding them compelled me to keep reading. The Elves' joys and sorrows were my own. I finished the book within days of starting it. Right away, my husband went out and bought me *The Fellowship of the Ring*.

During the night, I read; during the day, I searched the internet for information about the world created by Tolkien. I found there are many people who are totally absorbed by the tales, and I became part of that community. My outlook on life was shifting. I wanted to be one worthy of living in Middle-earth. I wanted to be wise, yet as strong as the Elves, to live a simple and happy life as hobbits do, and be as tenacious as the Dúnedain.

Achieving my goal of a Middle-earth life has been a work in progress. I began by allowing myself to be who I really am. A woman who was brought up by two loving parents: my father, a sweet, strong and wise provider for the family; my mother, a devoted matriarch, tender, and an excellent storyteller. Hence was born my love and joy for reading and weakness for powerful, yet sensitive, men.

I was a woman who rushed into creating a family at a very early age. I now accepted that my path was before me and one I must take. I could not turn back or give up; rather, I had to move forward and persist. Surrounded by my loved ones, I could not let time pass by without enjoying and appreciating my family. My marriage has been much sweeter and romantic; I would give up immortality for my husband, and I know he would fight grim battles for me.

Knowing that all of Middle-earth — its lands, realms, races and languages — came from the brilliant mind of one J.R.R. Tolkien inspired me to seek wider knowledge. It was out there somewhere, waiting for me to discover it. I began drawing again, having given it up for almost three years. I went back to college and took a writing class. Now I am in a stage of love. I can accept the beauty in humankind, the greatness of the Earth and universe, and most importantly, the light that lies within me.

In my daughters, I see the purity and intelligence of the women in Middle-earth. I intend to nurture this so they will grow up to be proud, spirited and happy women. Now ages five and two, they have already come to know and appreciate the timeless story of *The Lord of the Rings*. And so the tales go on....

Biography: Karime Limon-Rico. Born in Los Angeles, California in 1980, Karime Limon and her family resided in her birthplace until the age of three. Thereafter she grew up in Tijuana, Mexico, where she enjoyed a happy childhood along with many cousins. When she was nine, her younger brother was born and her family moved back to the United States. She now lives in San Diego with her husband and two children. Karime is currently enrolled in a community college and is an aspiring writer.

Lembas for the Soul

I Live in a World of Dreams
Anne Marie Gazzolo

My first exposure to *The Lord of the Rings*, although I did not know it at the time, was in 1980, when a beloved high school French teacher was leaving and I said, "May the Force be with you!" She responded with a very enthusiastic "Frodo lives!" I had absolutely no clue what she was talking about. I've wondered more than once why I still remember those words so vividly 25 years later. Over the course of all three *The Lord of the Rings* films, I was completely captivated by that beautiful hobbit and am now a completely unrepentant, full-fledged Frodoholic. I have *I Brake For Hobbits!* taped to the rear window of my car. I want to buy a home that's for sale near where I work, simply because it would be a perfect hobbit hole. I can so easily imagine Frodo and Bilbo being very happy there, and me with them!

I wonder when I am going to wear out the CD player in my car, since I am constantly playing *The Lord of the Rings* soundtracks. The last time I watched *Fellowship*, I laughed and had tears in my eyes, just from the sheer joy of watching Frodo be so beautiful and so happy. No one has affected me that deeply before. It is a bittersweet heartache to watch that happiness slowly disappear over the three films, but it is wonderful to see him smile, especially during the Quest, when he had so little to smile about. I love the first scene of him in the films, where he is reading a book beneath the tree — a hobbit after my own heart. If it weren't for those pesky bills, I would read and write all day myself.

Peter Jackson, the actors, screenwriters, Howard Shore and all the crew made such a wonderful adaptation of Professor Tolkien's sub-created world, adding their own powerful, personal touches as well. After *LOTR,* other films seem to fade into insignificance. *The Return of the King* filled a void in my life — one I didn't even know had existed until that moment. Elijah Wood's perfect performance was matched by everyone else in one big magnificent production. I don't watch just one of the films when the urge strikes. I have to watch them all over a succession of nights, because it's one big story. They are so well done, they make you want to start the next one right away.

The love between Frodo and Sam, portrayed so well in the films and even more so in the books, especially moved me. I've read *Fellowship* three times in the last year, and *The Two Towers* and *The Return of the King* twice. I am now reading *The Silmarillion,* the same haunting tales that Bilbo and Frodo read. I am awed by Professor Tolkien's complex, deeply woven tapestry of the early history of the Elves, men and Dwarves. Multiple Balrogs — what a time in which to live! And I thought *The Lord of the Rings* was rich in detail.

After watching the moving story of Cameron Duncan, watching the films and reading *The Silmarillion*, I felt inspired to write my own original fantasies. I have been writing much of my life, and now experience something similar to what the Professor described — that he was not creating a world purely out of his own imagination, but re-telling the history of a world that already existed, bringing a modern translation of ancient tales and songs. I hope to do the same.

I'm also having a ball writing about those marvelous hobbits and reading the reverent interpretations of other storytellers who emulate the master. Through them, I have been given a deeper appreciation of what gentle, loving souls the hobbits have. My heart has been broken more than once and tears have come to my eyes. It has been a *long* time since that has happened. As well as the master himself, these other writers have inspired me to deepen and strengthen my own stories.

But the most profound effect of my exposure to the Professor's works and Peter Jackson's wonderful re-telling of these tales came after I read a fan's story in which Sam never married; instead he devoted his post-Quest life to taking care of

131

Frodo. Now I am no longer perfectly happy being single. I long for my own Sam to marry, to be loved and to love that unconditionally. The most beautiful scene in the whole story is when Sam finds Frodo in the tower of Cirith Ungol. Sam thinks he could be happy for eternity just holding Frodo and watching over him. It shows the depth and purity of their love so perfectly. That humble gardener-turned-guardian-angel has been named Samwise the Brave, the Stouthearted, *Harthad Uluithiad* — Hope Unquenchable. Even more than all that, he is Samwise the Loving, a light to the world when all other lights go out.

Biography: Anne Marie Gazzolo. Anne Marie wishes she could live in the Shire near Frodo. She would spend her days reading and writing with her fellow book lover and scribe, watch Sam nurture his master and enjoy Merry and Pippin's antics. When she graduated to *LOTR* after 20+ years as a *Star Wars* fan, her sister aptly said, "She just switched one obsession for another." Or as Sean Astin remarked, "I was a huge *Star Wars* junkie ... but *The Lord of the Rings* ...[is] where my heart is." Please visit her at http://www.writers-haven.net/hobbity_love.htm.

Lembas for the Soul

Airs from an Ancient World
Dominique Lopez

When *The Lord of the Rings: The Fellowship of the Ring* premiered, I was vaguely interested in the movies. Of course, I had heard of the books, but had no desire to read them. My father bought the first installment on DVD and the moment I watched it, I was 'hooked'. My brain couldn't get enough of the beautiful costumes, the dialogue; and I loved the acting, too!

What most intrigued me was the exquisite music. I loved the way it was so wonderfully composed, and how well it fit with the scenes. I still wasn't a huge fan until *The Two Towers* came out and I heard *Forth Eorlingas*. This was the most moving piece of work I had ever experienced. It brought me to tears, and I knew that simple peak in the music when Eomer and his riders gallop down the hill to Helm's Deep changed me forever. I suppose it affected me in part due to my previous three years of playing flute. Since I have bought all of the soundtracks, I have almost worn them out, trying to discern every different instrument used and in what scene the piece was used. I constantly have one of the compositions in my head, and have often been given weird looks for conducting along with the musical variations.

It really wasn't just *LOTR* that changed my life, but rather specifically, it was Howard Shore and his beautiful music. In fact, I have been inspired so much that I am going to get a Master's degree in Music Composition and Theory so I can hopefully, one day, do what Howard Shore does now!

Biography: Dominique Lopez. "My name is Dominique Lopez and I am 18 years old. I will be attending college in the fall, where I will begin work on a Bachelor's degree in Film Scoring. I am a voracious reader and love picking apart musical pieces to discern every aspect, and then listening to the piece together again. I also am becoming more and more fluent in *LOTR* knowledge and hope soon to learn Elvish."

The Bard's Apprentice
Elizabeth Gottschalk

Many people have told me that my "obsession" with Tolkien is strange — "unnatural" even — as Sam would have said. People just do not seem to understand how a fantasy, a world that does not even truly exist outside of the mind of its creator and the imaginations of its readers, could change my life so drastically that I will be forever indebted to it.

I first started reading Tolkien when I was in eighth grade, before *The Lord of the Rings* movies came out. I immediately fell in love with the intricately plotted story, with the deep, vivid characters, with the rich, believable cultures, and with the brightly woven tapestry of the world. Soon, I was devouring anything Tolkien-related — books about Tolkien's life, books on his world views, and a 12-volume series on his process when writing the books set in Middle-earth. I loved them all. About the same time, I started spending a lot more time on the internet, searching for artwork and essays to read pertaining to Tolkien's life and works.

In the course of all this, I happened upon an internet community dedicated to Tolkien (www.tolkienonline.com). I had never been part of such a community before and I plunged into it. Deep friendships had always eluded me, and suddenly, that was no longer the case. I was surrounded by people with similar interests and passions, and as a result, found myself forming many strong friendships. People from all over the world, of all ages, became my friends. In fact, I met my best friend on Tolkien Online. We live more than an hour apart, but we do meet periodically in person, and I have never had such a deep friendship with anybody else. I have since become much more friendly and outgoing than I was. I find it much easier to approach others, and instead of always being quiet and timid, I am now far more outgoing. While it would have been unthinkable before, now I will often be the first to speak up in a group, or the first to introduce myself to a new person in a class.

The costumes in *The Fellowship of the Ring* inspired me to begin sewing again. When I was younger, my mother taught me how to sew, but I had not really done any sewing in years. But I wanted a cloak like the ones worn in the movie so, filled with a bit of trepidation—but a lot of excitement—I went to the fabric store again and bought a pattern and some fabric. By my present standards, that early cloak was shoddily done. But I enjoyed it so much that after making it, I decided to start making clothes again. Now, I make a large percentage of my own wardrobe. I have people asking me to make clothing for them as well. I have made dozens of costumes, and I am considered one of the most accomplished seamstresses at my school. I have even considered opening a small costume-making shop with my best friend.

But that isn't the end of Tolkien's influence on me. After reading his books, I decided to visit an archery range. I enjoyed archery so much that after only a few visits, I bought my own bow. Now I own two bows — a longbow and a recurve — and I go shooting frequently with my friends. I never would have visited that archery range, if not for Tolkien.

Most significantly, above all else, Tolkien kindled in me a love of writing. I think I have always, deep down, been a writer; I always loved creating worlds, and I always enjoyed developing them in my head. But I had never really entertained the idea of writing stories.

It started off as "fan fiction", original stories based in another author's world. I used Tolkien's characters and his Middle-earth as a basis to weave my own tales. After less than a year of that, I realized that fan fiction would never be able to satisfy me — I wanted to write about my own worlds. I wanted to be able to create from scratch.

So I started writing original fantasy. And I love it! It is absolutely my favorite pastime, after reading. I love to write — I am in the middle of a novel and about a dozen different short stories. They are what I do when I am bored, when I am sad, when I am happy, when I am busy. I think I would have begun to write eventually, years down the road. I have too much creativity in me for it to stay bottled up forever. But who knows how long it would have taken? This way, I started writing years and years earlier. I have so much more time to learn, and to get better than I otherwise would have been.

And I owe that to Tolkien. All of it. My inspiration and desire to write might have come later, but now I have that much more time to enjoy it.

Perhaps now you can understand why it isn't so strange to say that one man's work—and fantasy at that—has completely made over my life.

Elizabeth Gottschalk

Lembas For the Soul

Elf-obsessed

Loredana (Dana) Tonello

I read the opening chapter of my fledgling fantasy novel and listened to strangers critiquing my writing at the Santa Barbara Writers Conference. They liked it ... a lot. I was here by lucky chance and a shared love of Tolkien with a lady who believed in me. None of this would have happened had it not been for a certain Elf.

A diehard sci-fi/fantasy reader since childhood, reality bored me. Imagination soared. I lost myself in other worlds, joining with the characters, fighting alongside them, riding dragons, discovering new planets and peoples. My obsession for the fantastic never waned. That my working life began in a library helped fuel the obsession. I 'met' the Tolkien crew in my 20s, collecting discarded library books through the periodic sales by the State Library of Western Australia. My first four years' salary went into the purchase of books, especially *The Lord of the Rings* trilogy. Those Elves ... there was a cool, logical, timeless quality to those guys. Much as Mr. Spock had always been my *Star Trek* favourite, so Legolas became my Elf obsession. But I was quite unprepared for the 20-year reunion via Peter Jackson's films.

When I saw Jackson's interpretation of my beloved Elves, I almost accepted him as my new God. The ethereal beauty of Orlando Bloom embodied everything my Legolas had been. My Elf obsession became all-consuming. Desperate for images of this paragon of Elven Perfection, I trawled the internet and chanced across a site called "Hot-Elf"...aptly named, I thought, as I downloaded image after image. I noticed the site also had a forum and message board to talk to the fellow Elf-obsessed. I joined. I quickly gained popularity for my Photoshop creations involving my picture cleverly spliced with either Orlando Bloom or Legolas. Four months later a lady from Santa Barbara happened upon this site, offering to edit people's fan fictions and assist with Elvish languages. Her fiancé had been killed in Iraq. I replied to her topic, offering condolences for her loss and presuming on her to edit/look over a short story I had begun. We continued to interact on the forum, and discovered we both had a snarky wit and wicked sense of humor.

She was older than anyone on the site, beating me by more than ten years, and we laughingly called ourselves the site's "fossils". Soon, though, she became "auntie" to dozens of girls on the site, some with real problems in their real lives — cutting, depression, anorexia, ADHD, as well as the usual problems teens face with school, parental units and boys. Between the two of us, and some sensible peers, we created a sisterhood and support network where the girls could freely discuss their problems without judgment or derision. "Auntie" would provide spiritual guidance and advice, whereas little heathen, street-wise, been-there-done-that me would provide practical or ludicrous solutions to their problems.

I sent her the 20 pages of the story I had commenced, uncertain if I was any good. She sent back hard copy covered in blue scribbles and two pages of typed notes. She was a professional writer and editor, and she told me not to despair at the amount of blue on the pages. She said I had done remarkably well, as you could still see some white on the pages. I took those two pages of style notes to heart. My next chapters were less fraught with errors. The story grew; more chapters, fewer errors, and developed with twists and turns not previously envisioned. I created a timeline, and my story paralleled Tolkien's meticulously. I had heard how the fan-fic community savaged people who did not stay true to Tolkien's world or characters. My last submission contained only four editorial errors: three commas and a redundancy. Auntie was pleased that her *padawan* had learned her craft and listened to her teachings. But she offered me a greater challenge: we would write a collaborative fiction.

138

It's one thing to write by yourself. You have all the ideas and know where you want the story to go, but to continue the story after someone has already begun it seemed daunting. She was a professional ... I had to keep up with *her*? She sent me an outline, where the story would go, how it would progress. My first chapter was a bare two and a half pages long. As the story developed, we would email each other the chapters for perusal prior to posting, and also to brainstorm new ideas, characters or situations. The time difference between Australia and the U.S. never presented a problem, as I was online during work hours, toggling back and forth from my graphic design day job. Auntie was the night owl/freelance writer working from home. We even phoned each other and discussed our 'epic', finding nuances previously overlooked. The story evolved over months. We even interspersed holidays and real-life situations within the story. Tolkien's creations had become our individual muses and they would whisper in our ears and take us with them on incredible journeys.

Then Auntie asked me how much airfare was from Australia to the USA. I asked her why she wanted to know, and she informed me she had organized a scholarship to the Santa Barbara Writers' Conference for me in 2005. I laughed and said, "I'm not a writer." She said, "Yes, you are." I said, "Fan fiction doesn't count, I can't publish it." But Auntie said, "You're already published on the internet. Now, create your own story. You're ready."

I saved my money, booked leave from work and began my own fantasy fiction, ever aware of the Tolkien influence, but creating my own universe. The heroine of my piece is derived from one of my Tolkien-inspired RPG characters, interspersed with liberal doses of my own snarky, hyperactive, adrenalin-addicted nature. The hero, of course, is tall, blue-eyed and blond-haired, fairer than mortal man deserves to be. He had to be, to create my own Legolas.

Lembas For the Soul

Biography: Loredana (Dana) Tonello. Born in 1961 in Perth, Western Australia, Dana is a graphic designer by day and a writer by night. She loves Elves, bungee jumping, snowboarding, flying, surfing, yoga, dragons, photography and archery. She drives a 1991 Alfa Romeo as fast as she can get away with and owns three-quarters of her townhouse. Shopping and travel are her weaknesses. She is fluent in Italian, knows Sindarin and basic French. Take her to a Thai restaurant if you want to impress her. Dana wishes to be reincarnated as Orlando Bloom's pet. She is a true Gemini.

Sea Longing

Cales from the Green Dragon

Ring-a-holics
Tracy and Julia Reisinger

End of January, 2004

Our names are Julia and Tracy, and we are *Lord of the Rings-*aholics.

We were talking about it yesterday as we were on our way to see *The Return of the King* for the eighth time. We saw it on Saturday and then again on Sunday this weekend. Twice now, we've seen it twice in one day. We have seen it every weekend since it was released, with the exception of last weekend, when we visited our parents in another state. Each time, we stay until the credits are finished, because we like the sketches and the closing music.

Just about every day for the last several months, we each go to *The Return of the King* website or *theOneRing.net* website to read about the movie, the cast, awards being given to it, and so on. Our friends, Allen and Tina, gave us two six-foot-tall cardboard movie cutouts of our favorite character, Legolas the Elf. We stayed up way past our bedtime last night watching the Golden Globe Awards to see if our movie won best picture, musical score, director, and song (it swept all categories!).

But we're not entirely insane. While we go to the websites every day, at least we aren't *posting* to the websites. While we go see the movie every weekend, at least we aren't dressing up like the characters, as some fans have been. We're not *that* geeky.

While we have twin cardboard cutouts of Legolas, it's not like we bought them ourselves. (I mean, we're not going to turn away a Christmas present from friends.) That they are prominently displayed in both our living room and our workout room so we can see them all the time means nothing.

This Sunday, as we were getting ready to go to the movie again, we realized we were out of cash and had to raid the change jar to get enough to pay for the tickets. As we were walking from the car to the theater, Julia sniffed (not unlike a cocaine addict) and said, "Do you have the cash?" under her breath.

That's when we realized we might have a problem. All we could think about was that we can't go again until next weekend, and how many more times we would be able to see it before it leaves the theater. Then we're cold turkey until the DVD comes out. In the last three weeks, we've watched the whole trilogy three times the whole way through (with the first two movies on DVD and the third in the theater). Maybe some type of intervention *is* needed.

Update: End of May, 2005

When you need an intervention, it's not good to go to friends who are just as addicted as you are. Far from trying to help us break this addiction, they continue to feed us with it. The same friends who gave us the twin cardboard cutouts of Legolas have since bought us *The Lord of the Rings* DVD *Trivial Pursuit* game. We spent the equivalent of three days not playing the game, but going through all the DVD questions so we could see all the scenes.

Those same friends drove with us from a Seattle Mariners game back to Portland last summer. We spent over three hours in the car reading *The Lord of the Rings* Trivial Pursuit questions out loud to stay awake. The problem with this game is that if you know all the answers, you can win the game on your first try. Between all four of us, we have a correct response rate of over 95 percent.

Lembas for the Soul

We of course took the day off work to purchase and watch *The Return of the King* Extended Edition DVD when it came out in December, and we have practically memorized the *Day in the Life of a Hobbit* in the special interview appendixes. In December of 2004, we were almost forced to quit cold turkey when we couldn't find a *Lord of the Rings* day-by-day calendar. We found one at the last minute, feeding Tina's addiction as well by getting one for her. We keep them on our desks at work. Tina will email and say things like "Mr. February 5th is looking great today." One shot was of Legolas with a smirk on his face. Of course we laughed, because we knew the next words out of his mouth from that exact scene in the movie: "A diversion!" Tina said we were sick, but we don't take any criticism from the woman who can distinguish Orthanc (the tower itself) from Isengard (the place). She should talk.

Now that the extended edition of the final movie is out, we know the end is near. We will be forced to deal with our addiction and suffer until Peter Jackson can wrestle the rights to *The Hobbit* from the tangled web of whoever controls them. Until then, we stick with watching the extra features over and over, planning our eventual trip to New Zealand, the adopted country of Middle-earth, and hoping that when we must deal with our disease, it can be later rather than sooner. Always later.

Biography: Tracy and Julia Reisinger. Tracy and Julia Reisinger are twin sisters who share a house in Portland, Oregon, with their two cats. When not watching *The Lord of the Rings:* Director's Cut DVD and appendixes, they listen to *The Lord of the Rings* books on tape during their lunch breaks at work. Sometimes, you can never get too much of a great thing.

The Fellowship
of the Line Party
Kelly L. Silvey

December 16, 2003: a day (and night) that will live in infamy. No one who attended our line party remained unchanged. Some were scarred for life. What follows is an accurate account of what really happened during the long hours of the Las Cruces, New Mexico, *Return of the King* Line Party.

The journey began many weeks before the actual date of the release. Careful planning was needed to ensure our gathering would be memorable. With the grace of Iluvatar, my friend Seth was able to grasp the coveted *theOneRing.net* line party administration duties. Many signed up to attend, but the real fun began when Seth, Loren and I, the masterminds, began to advertise our party around town.

We would walk around our town of 90,000 people, tearing off fraternity fliers and replacing them with fliers that Seth and Loren had created. Some of their fliers were simple and gave basic information about the party. However, some should be preserved for generations to come. One depicted Seth and Loren in Las Vegas, in cheap suits, groovin' in a parking lot with a huge animated figure of Gandalf the Grey in their wake. As Seth and Loren advertised, I worked diligently in the kitchen, preparing a hearty yet delicately flavored *lembas* bread recipe. I knew our hunger would be great during our long encampment.

Our advertising and baking complete, we waited anxiously for the day of doom. We met at the theater on a cold winter's morning. The pale yellow sun could not warm us, but we were not deterred. We had arisen early and waited patiently for the tickets to go on sale. Others were before us, safe behind the canvas walls of their Helm's Deep tent, yet ultimately, we would prevail.

145

The tickets bought, we made the long and arduous 20-step march to where the real line began. We were of the first to be in line — others were daunted by our dedication. And then, the waiting began. Like Pippin waiting on the edge of war, we tried to keep our spirits up. A radio station had come to hand out prizes for those who could spout out Tolkien trivia. I was pushed forward by my friends, and unwillingly stepped up to the microphone.

"Who helped the hobbits out of the barrows?" I was asked. "Tom Bombadil!" [Applause] "What was the name of Aragorn's sword before it was reforged?" "Um...it was Anduril afterwards ... Narsil!" [More applause] My prize was a copy of *The Fellowship* on DVD: not too shabby.

The day wore on. I was called to do my duty as a Mearas trainer and therapist (a.k.a. work as an Equine Assisted Psychotherapist) for a few hours. Little did I know that a black steed of Sauron would step on my foot and break my toe. And yet my will was set, and only death would break it. I gathered some food from Ithilien for my friends — who knew Gondor had Wendy's? — and traveled back to the line. We took a little food of Gondor, and then the *lembas* bread I had made. Yes, my elven blood flowed strong that day, and all those around us were soon asking for more *lembas*.

The day waned; darkness and cold fell like a shadow on our hearts. And yet we would not give in. Seth and Loren set up *The Lord of the Rings Risk* and began to play. I brought out my cloak and some blankets. It was bone-chillingly cold that December day, and we were reminded of The Fellowship as they battled cruel Caradhras. If only we had some of Gandalf's *miruvor* to warm our cold spirits. I rummaged around and retrieved the coveted *lembas* bread. Its light, golden-sweet flavor heartened us against the freezing air.

And then, disaster. As Loren got up to go to the bathroom, an orcish man, swarthy in appearance, followed him in to tell him to take off his hat, which happened to have a very funny bumper sticker on it. Loren did not think the swarthy orc-man was serious, so he laughed. I looked up as Loren returned outside, just in time to see the orc-man step up and punch him in the mouth. Blood was dripping at my feet. I screamed. The orc-man ran off before we could catch him.

Loren was bleeding profusely, and swayed before I could help him sit down. I ran inside to get some towels and call the police. There was no way Loren could remain in line. We were almost defeated. Seth volunteered to take him to the nearest hospital for stitches while I held the fort. Like Eowyn at Dunharrow I sat, feeling helpless. There was nothing more I could do.

The minutes wore on. It was getting close...the board was set, and the pieces were moving. I tried calling Seth in vain. I felt no hope of victory. There was no way they could get back in time. To pass the hours, I made a get well card out of scraps of paper. Well over 50 signatures were on the card by showtime. The goodness of men was shown in those hours. Everyone was worried; everyone was cheering for my friends.

And then, a light in dark places! They made it back just in the nick of time! The line was moving indoors when Loren reappeared, swollen-lipped and unable to talk. Wounded like Frodo, taken care of by Seth like dear Samwise, Loren was able to finish the journey. We got decent seats in the theater, feeling a surge of pride in our tenacity throughout the long, wearisome day, and focused on the reason we had all been brought together: *The Return of the King*.

The film was amazing, but our Fellowship during our long wait was the stuff of legend. Everything described above actually happened. The *lembas* bread, the cut lip — all of these events played out like the great stories of our time.

Biography: Kelly L. Silvey. Kelly (also known as Kelly of Luthien) is a school social worker living in Las Cruces, NM. Known as the resident Tolkien geek by her friends, Kelly can frequently be found listening to the funky beats of *The Lords of the Rhymes*, her favorite hobbit rap group. Kelly enjoys reading, camping and hunting for Silmarils.

Lembas for the Soul

The Pass of Caradhras
jon Baril, TK

"I don't care if it snows! I'm going!"

And I meant it. Rachel and I had been planning for weeks to walk to the movie theater to see *The Two Towers* and no alleged snowstorm was going to stop us. The timing was perfect: President's Day, the start of February vacation. With Rachel out of school, we would have a national holiday to stroll that mile or two and get some much-needed exercise. We would soak in the wonder of Peter Jackson's movie for the fifth time, trying to surpass last year's seven viewings of *The Fellowship of the Ring*. Then Rachel and I would spend the walk back home from the theater discussing the problems of Faramir.

The day was so anticipated that when weathermen began forecasting a blizzard, we blocked it from our minds. After all, New England weather is horribly unpredictable. Even if it snowed, we would still walk to the film. And if the snow was truly as bad as they predicted, we would just call home and ask to be picked up. No matter what nature would throw at us, Rachel and I were determined to walk up there that Monday morning in February.

Still, as the snow blew into my face and I lost all feeling in my nose, I couldn't help wondering if I'd made the right decision. The snow melted on my glasses as they fogged up, and it was difficult to see. Thankfully, the wind was not blowing too strongly.

More snow, more wind, more cold. The walk took almost twice as long as usual.

"I'm *really* cold," said Rachel. "I can't feel my face!"

"That's all right, we're almost there," I said. After crossing the street and taking the sidewalk through the trees, we saw the glorious sign of the Framingham AMC Theater. Moving as quickly as possible, we arrived at the front doors, wiped our glasses, shook out our hair, and entered with exhausted, victorious sighs. "We made it!" I said. "Two for *The Lord of the Rings*, please."

Three hours later, we stepped back into the cold. As we crossed the parking lot, I noticed how deep the snow had become.

148

Reaching into my pocket, I pulled out my phone and called home, but the reply was not one I had expected.

"I'm all snowed in here," Dad said. "Just start walking. I'll find you when I can get out."

As Dad picked up the shovel, Rachel and I headed out into the white wasteland before us. Snow piles rose to my knees and higher. We started trudging down the sidewalk as best we could, sinking each foot in, step by step, hoping always for a stretch of someone else's prints to walk in.

Fifteen minutes later, my phone rang. It was Dad. "Well, the idiot snowplow pushed a bunch of snow back into the driveway. I'm still going to be awhile. Get as far as Chi-Chi's and I'll meet you there as soon as possible." The delay was disheartening, but now we had an objective, a destination.

I noticed Rachel struggling. She is smaller than me, and I turned back periodically to see her jumping into my footprints to ease her walk. Amid her grunts, it was clear that my strides were too much for her. The snow was higher than expected, and the constant stress on my legs was wearisome. I had the presence of mind to put on two pairs of pants before leaving the house that morning, but Rach wore only one, and it was clear she was freezing.

After several falls and difficult snow dunes, I resolved to take a different approach for Rachel's sake. I turned back to her and said, in my best Ian McKellen impression, "We must take the pass of Caradhras!"

With all the force I could muster, I drove my legs through the snow, dragging away all I could. I recalled how Tolkien described Boromir swimming through the snows of Caradhras, and tried my best to emulate him as I cleared a path for Rachel. It was not perfect, but she could move more easily as the snow blew down. When snow was piled too high, I would use my hands, while each foot dragged along whatever passed for ground.

"We cannot stay here!" I continued in full *Lord of the Rings* mode. "This will be the death of the hobbits!" I strode on, and she followed.

"I'm a hobbit!" she said. I repeated as many snatches of dialogue as I could recall. As the wind blew, I said things like, "There is a fell voice on the air." Rachel would chime in too, and we laughed as we pressed on. Remembering how The Fellowship fared in the snow gave us a focus.

There came a point where we were gladly able to break out of the heap and walk in the street beside the Route 9 sidewalk. The roads were practically empty. Chi-Chi's Mexican Restaurant was nearby. Suddenly, out of the snowy mist, came the shapes of three huge plows, one in each lane. They came in perfect succession, and we realized we had to move. I'd hoped they would see us and avoid us, but they drove on, uncaring. There was nowhere to go. I wished I could walk on snow like Legolas, because I dreaded returning to it. After a moment's thought, we both jumped back onto the snow-drifted sidewalk, pushing forward and cursing the plows.

Not long after, we reached the relative haven of Chi-Chi's parking lot and soon our father arrived. We had survived the blinding snows and the cruel plowmen, returning with delirious smiles and snowy clothes. As we warmed up at home and recounted our adventures, I thought about how we were like Frodo and Sam; how, despite all obstacles, we kept going, because we were holding on to something. We remember the day fondly, when our will was set and only death would break it.

Biography: jon Baril, TK. Jon is a recent graduate of Emerson College who dabbles in many things, but presently fancies himself a writer. He has been an avid reader from a young age, and introduced himself to Tolkien in the third grade, reading *The Hobbit* several times, as well as *The Fellowship of the Ring*. He has since declared *The Lord of the Rings* to be the best book ever written in English, and continues to re-read it periodically, often in a self-devised chronological fashion. jon currently lives in Framingham, Massachusetts, where he still walks to the movies, even in inclement weather.

Lembas for the Soul

Getting in Touch with Your Inner Gollum
Celandine Took

It is a truth universally acknowledged that sooner or later, every true *Lord of the Rings* fan will be tempted to do a Gollum impression. In fact, there are uncounted thousands who are *not even Ringers* who have attempted this feat.

I can personally attest to this because I live with someone who must surely hold the record for the worst Gollum impression in the land. My husband, who is *soooo* not into Tolkien, has overheard enough dialogue from *The Two Towers* and *The Return of the King* to try out his own version of Gollum. Even the dogs fled the room and cowered under furniture when they heard his creepy but pathetic impression.

So, my fellow Ringers, now is the moment for truth. Who, in the bitter watches of the night, has not called for *The Precious*?

It starts innocuously enough, adding extra s's here and there: orcses, jacketses, extended edition DVDses. It creeps insidiously into your conversations before you become aware of it. Your emails begin to have Gollum-esque riffs and rants. When you are asking for something, a *we wants it* slips out. Soon, when someone displeases you, you say they are *wicked, tricksy, false.* When you're hungry, it's *no crunchable birdses.* And when someone *really* gets up your nose, you are heard to mutter *filthy little thieves!*

People begin to avoid you when your conversation is sprinkled with "my love" or "my Preciousss" at inappropriate moments. Harmless enough, right?

However, singing Gollum's fish song and asking the staff at *Long John Silver's*, "What's taters, Precious?" may result in an embarrassing public use of restraints. Sadly, there is no known cure except, perhaps, a whack to the side of the head by an acutely annoyed friend or family member.

151

Lembas for the Soul

I have had some experience of this phenomenon myself. When the soundtrack for *The Return of the King* came out, I haunted the stores for a month for a copy that had Legolas or Aragorn on the cover. All I could find were copies with Icky Old Denethor on the front. *Eeuuw*. Who wants one of those?

Then one day after the Christmas rush I walked into *Best Buy* and there he was: the Perfect Elf! I snatched the cd from the rack and held it pressed to my heart for a moment. "It's mine, my own...my Preciousss." Sure, I got plenty of strange looks from the other customers, but the Precious was mine.

Yet the supreme moment for my inner Gollum came the morning after *The Return of the King* made film history at the Academy Awards. I raced to work, eager to share my joy with my geek co-workers, and let's be honest, to rub it in for the naysayers.

I rushed through the staff entrance and out through the workroom. Then I twirled through the Circulation Area, chanting, "The Preciousss! The Preciousss!"

Some of my co-workers stared aghast, while my fellow Ringers laughed. I continued to dance and spin across the floor, still calling to the Precious and chortling with glee. I finally came to a stop in front of the Reference Desk. "Woo-hoo!" I whooped. "*A clean sweep!*"

By now astute readers will have discerned that I work at A Library. Some may be appalled by such unseemly behavior in a library, a place for quiet study, reading and reflection. I hasten to assure them that this happened before public hours. Some may believe that in these instances we should have been dignified and gracious, smiling and nodding slightly to acknowledge our victory. And so it may be for some future celebration. But as I thought then, it shall not be *this day*—this day, we *gloat!*

So there you have the true tale of how The Precious Dance came to be. Some may also think the story ends there. But no, there are many paths in Middle-earth that we have yet to travel....

After the Oscars, the naysayers sulked, saying, "*The Lord of the Rings* movies are now history. It's time to move on."

"No way," we said, "the Platinum Extended DVD Edition doesn't come out until December!"

And so it was that *LOTR* fever reigned until the release of the Extended Edition of *ROTK* and continues scarcely diminished to this present day. In fact, a geek friend and I were recently discussing the promised SuperDuper Expanded DVD set. We know we'll be there on Release Day, cash in hand.

We laughed, imagining a distant future in some senior community. I'll come hobbling down the hall with my cane. "Glorwynedheliriel," I'll call out, "the 25th Anniversary Mega-Humungous *Lord of the Rings* DVD boxed set is being released today!"

Glorwynedheliriel hastens to catch up, the wheels of her walker squeaking on the linoleum floor. "The one with all the lost footage they found in that old warehouse on Stone Street?"

"That's it! I'll finally get to see that post-coronation footage. Do you know how many years I've waited to see Legolas strolling through the woods of Ithilien? I wrote to PJ back in Aught Four asking for it." I frown. "I don't know why it's taken them this long to release it."

We jostle some old people out of our way as we head outside. "Make way for the Shield Grannies of Rohan!"

Brandishing my cane, I dispatch our customary driver—who had an orcish air about him any way—and commandeer the Assisted Living Center van. As we drive off, I shout, "*Forth Eorlingas!*"

Riding shotgun, Glorwynedheliriel asks, "How many *LOTR* DVD sets have we bought so far?"

"At least 8."

"I think it's closer to a dozen." She squints into the bright Arizona sun. "Don't they come out every other year?"

"That's right. They trade off years with the *Star Wars* franchise."

We careen through the traffic, only running one or two drivers with slow reflexes off the road. Eventually we screech into the parking lot, stopping crosswise in a disabled parking space. We scramble out of the van (well, if one can actually *scramble* with a walker) and hurry inside to finally come to a halt before the pyramid of the 3D *LOTR* 25th Anniversary set boxes.

As we stand there in awe, our eyes gleam green. Then we share knowing smiles. *The Precious still has us.*

Biography: Celandine Took. Celandine lives in a *mathom*-cluttered hole in the East Farthing with her gardener husband, Rudigar, five dogs, a flock of eccentric chickens and one extremely cantankerous goat. She enjoys creating fan fiction based on *The Red Book of Westmarch,* and her main ambition is to climb one of the White Towers beyond the Far Downs and see past the veils of mist to the shores of The Undying Lands.

The Grey Ship

The Road Goes Ever On

Mount Sunday
Ravenna of Buckland

The road to Mount Sunday bounces the SUV, although the driver — my tour guide — is careful. Even on a day strangely warm for mid-July (mid-winter here, as I keep reminding myself), ice lines the lakes, and frost makes the high grass crunchy when we stop so that I can take pictures before we get to our destination. Although this isn't my first trip to New Zealand, it's my first time in this part of South Island, not far from Methven, but away from the busier ski slopes. In fact, on this sunny Tuesday morning, I spot no other vehicles once we leave the paved motorways and head down the gravel road.

Finally, I see a ribboning river below the relatively higher hill where we're driving, and I know that we're getting close. The late morning sun renders the river silver, so that it already seems like part of a snapshot instead of a curving, carving part of the living landscape. Before this trip, I somehow reduced this magnificent point where the plains meet the mountains to a series of images from Jackson's masterpiece: Éowyn standing alone, searching the plains for something, someone she did not yet know; Merry watching from another precipice as his beloved cousin rides away from him; Aragorn smoking a pipe on a starry evening when the landscape is washed blue/white. To see these images come alive for me, with me — that is magic in itself.

My guide tells me that around the next bend I'll be able to see Mount Sunday. Leaning forward in anticipation, I look for the rocky hill as he slows the vehicle. "There it is," he points out, and I see what seems to be a small, singular mountain on a plain in the middle of more impressive snowy peaks. After I play tourist by taking a few long shots, my driver presses a button on the

156

dash, and the soundtrack to *The Two Towers* fills the SUV. We travel off the regular road and drive cross country toward the base of Mount Sunday. I'm here at last. *Welcome to Edoras.*

As we wind our way ever closer, I learn that distances in New Zealand can be deceiving. This privately owned land, to which my guide has special clearance, is vast, at least in my urban U.S.-oriented mind. The little stream that doesn't look impressive from the road suddenly seems swift and wide (and undoubtedly cold if we get stuck) as we drive through it. Only later, when from the top of Mount Sunday I look down again on the stream, do I realize that this is where Gandalf rode, taking poor Pippin with him to Minas Tirith. For some people, that might not be a thrill. For someone who's read the books many times and seen the movie lots more, this is an important day.

Mount Sunday is much more impressive up close, too, as I discover when I huff and puff my way to the summit. A few stray goats undoubtedly laugh as I discover just how out of shape one can become walking only on flat stretches of land. But the view is worth being out of breath. While I stand, hands on knees, and breathe the clean air (one of the few times in my life I remember that air doesn't have to smell like anything), my guide points out the highlights.

Here in the center, on a solid stretch of rocky ground, is where the Golden Hall was built and where the stables once stood. He points toward the east across the brown grass. There the people of Rohan wound their way across the plain when they left Edoras for Helm's Deep, a river of refugees following their king to an uncertain fate. When I turn around, toward the west, in the distance I see where Aragorn rode up for his first view of Helm's Deep. The break in the mountainside is obvious, and my guide explains that the fortress was digitally inserted into the film. In my mind, though, I can see what Aragorn saw, a hidden refuge well protected by the gray rocks, well chosen because it offers a clear view of approaching armies.

Yes, again I have to play tourist and have my picture taken at the place where Éowyn looked over Rohan and first saw

Aragorn. I take more photos as I stand where Merry focused on Pippin's ever-diminishing form as Shadowfax sprinted away (or at least where the tower was built to provide him that vantage point). No matter how many pictures I snap, my poor panoramic shots can't compare to pivoting to take in 360 degrees of living, breathing beauty. Nowhere else have I felt land so alive, both welcoming and awe-inducing.

Of course, no evidence of film crews, or Rohirrim, remains, except in my memory. But the country is a star is its own right and well worth the trip, not only from Christchurch to Methven to Mount Sunday, but also from Orlando to Los Angeles to South Island. "I came, I saw, I conquered" doesn't apply here. I came and I saw, but I was conquered by the sheer loveliness of it all — sun glimmering off the snow-dusted peaks to the west, long stretches of plain surrounded by walls of mountains leading to the taller sections of the Southern Alps, streams wandering across the grassland, even the brown tufts of grass that my guide comments proudly were replanted if they had been moved to accommodate film sets. New Zealanders are proud of their land, and I feel pride that the filmmakers took care not to trample it just to make a movie, no matter how grand.

More important, my life becomes simple this day. Eating lunch with amiable companions, all of us sitting on camp chairs and just taking in the glorious scenery — what more would I ever need? The best of life is all around me, not only the sanctity of nature, but the shared pleasure of being with people who feel the same way.

So when I watch *The Two Towers* or *The Return of the King* and see Edoras, I can picture myself on Mount Sunday on a perfect winter's day and rejoice that not only can people see such beauty on film, or, if they're lucky, visit in person, but that it exists. I was brought up with a belief in heaven on Earth, but it took a pilgrimage to Mount Sunday, in the South Island of New Zealand, before I found it.

Lembas for the Soul

Biography: Ravenna of Buckland. Ravenna likes to travel far from the Shire but enjoys discussing all things hobbit, whether at home or abroad. She is particularly pleased to make new friends through a shared love of *The Lord of the Rings*.

The Old Forest

Sofia Makrinou

During the summer of 2004, I was with my husband and kids at our summerhouse on one of the very few green mountains of my country, a mountain rich in myths and ruined cities from our past. We have regularly visited this part of Greece for the last 15 years, but apparently we had not explored it well enough....

One morning in mid August, we decided to make a grand *tournee* through the villages nearby instead of going to the beach, because the sky was dark with clouds and a heavy, warm rain soon started to fall. By chance — or perhaps not — the previous afternoon I had baked my *lembas* bread (a delicious sweet-and-salty cake which takes about six to eight hours to prepare), so I put it in a mobile fridge along with apples, peaches, grapes, and a lot of water. Then we took off in our car.

We had seen most of the mountain villages by midday and had our coffee and traditional sweet figs in a wonderful square under the platans (sycamores) which protected us from the rain. When the rain stopped, a bright, hot sun quickly dried the leaves and grass, and also made us thirsty. On the way home, we took a road we had driven once or twice before, but now we were searching for a place to stop the car and have our lunch, because the children were really hungry.

A rough, earthen track led away from the main road to an open and flat place, where only thyme and rocks grew, which is normal for my country. In the distance, two horses were tied in a tuft of trees. A tiny trickle of water made a path between the rocks and instinctively we followed it. It followed the slope, and as it went down it grew larger, until it became a stream. The platans were thicker and bigger. Here we passed under a leafy arch and found ourselves on a green forested slope, completely protected from sight. The trees were tall and leafy. Their roots

160

massive and curling above the ground, the trees drew up as much water as they could from the little stream.

We saw tumbled stones from something that must have been a house at least 200 years ago, and more recently it had served as a shepherd's shelter for sheep and goats. There was also another ruin, a sort of stone bridge which stood next to — but not across — the stream. Later, we discovered it was a cellar, not a bridge, which now was half out of the ground. It still had some huge clay jars for wine and oil in it.

So we sat on top of that cellar and ate our *lembas* and fruit with our legs hanging down to the water. The children ran about and climbed on the huge twisted roots, reciting phrases from the book like, "Come on, Mr. Frodo, a few more steps!" or "You shall not pass!" I was really convinced I was in the Old Forest, carelessly eating my *lembas* and having my young hobbits running around me. For children at five and eight years old in their summer short pants and long hair do really look like hobbits!

It was an unforgettable day for me, and once more I believed my dreams can really come to life, if I want it so very much. And I do. Wherever I go, I will always look for Middle-earth and its people ...

Biography: Sofia Makrinou. "I am Sofia. I was born 34 years ago in Athens, Hellas, where I still live, now with my husband and two children, a girl and a boy, the joys of my life. I studied graphic design and I have been working with my husband as free-lancers for eight years. I speak fluent French and well enough English and Italian. I'm currently working on my Spanish, Quenya and Sindarin, along with Tengwar ...

"I practice miniature painting and have had two personal exhibitions with painted eggs. I carve mother of pearl, which I began after seeing the trilogy and getting to know New Zealand and its people better. I am a fanatic reader, mostly of classic literature, and I had not read *LOTR* until I saw *The Two Towers* by chance (or maybe not so) in December 2002. From that day on, I have read from it practically every day. I love to cook and here is my famous *lembas* bread recipe.

Lembas For the Soul

You will need:

500gr flour = 2 cup + 1 tbsp
45gr yeast   = 3 tbsp + 1 tsp
6 eggs
¼ of a cup of tea sugar (white sugar)
1 teaspoon of salt
250gr of good, pure butter = 9 oz

Mix the leaven with 4 spoonfuls of warm (not hot) water and leave it for 10 minutes to become like a cream. Then mix the flour, the salt, the wet leaven and the eggs (which we had previously beaten well in a bowl) well. Melt the butter with the sugar in low heat and add it to the rest. Turn and work for at least 10 minutes, until the mixture is homogenized. Cover the bowl with a plastic film and leave it in a room in stillness for 6 to 8 hours to rise. It really grows, so make sure the bowl is big enough! Bake it in a buttered and floured large baking pan in a preheated oven in 200C/400F for 20 minutes, or until the surface becomes light brown. *Bon appetit*!

Journey to the West
Gwendolyn Van Hout Knechtel

"I envy you." He handed me the worn paperbacks. "I'll never forget the first time I read *The Lord of the Rings*."

"Guess that means I'll always remember the spring of 1974." I carefully balanced the three books by J.R.R. Tolkien. "If these covers are any indication, looks like a great fantasy read."

"I hope you'll love them as much as I do, Gwendolyn."

"This must be an important occasion. You rarely use my entire name."

The 21-year-old Language House resident grinned. "It is. Consider *The Lord of the Rings* part of your college education — one that will stay with you the rest of your life."

My smile reflected his. "I hope that will be a long time — I'm just 19."

"I hope so too. A long life … together."

"Only time will tell, Grant. But whatever our future, thank you for this gift."

* * *

"Hard to believe it's been over 30 years since I first read *The Lord of the Rings*. And now they're movies." I look at the calendar. "Speaking of movies, the extended DVD edition of *The Return of the King* comes out this month. Want to fix a hobbit meal and do a family *LOTR* night?"

"Sounds like a good way to begin the holidays," my geologist husband replies and gives me a hug. "Well, off to have fun with dirt."

We kiss. Linger. "I love you, Gwen."

"And I love you, Grant." From my vertically challenged four feet, 11 inches, I reach up to his nearly six feet for a last squeeze. "Drive safe."

"You, too." And he is out the door.

I return to the kitchen as thoughts pour in like the coffee streaming into my travel mug.

At 50, married for 27 years with a high school-aged son and a daughter in community college who still lives at home, I have a list of worries. At the top is having my 84-year-old father in hospice care and my mother, his primary care giver, dealing with the decline of her husband of 52 years. With various health issues affecting loved ones and attending too many memorial services, aging is definitely not for wimps!

"The road goes ever on and on..." As Bilbo's song spins through my head, my mind whirls me to work where my office space is surrounded by *The Lord of the Rings* sayings, magnets, a calendar. Displayed prominently is a favorite quote from *The Fellowship of the Ring* that keeps life in perspective.

"I wish it need not have happened in my time," said Frodo.

"So do I," said Gandalf, "and so do all who live to see such times. But that is not for them to decide. All we have to decide is what to do with the time that is given us."

At times it seems impossible to decide what to do with the time given! The challenges of my parents' situation and balancing family, work and volunteering keep my stress levels high. To cope, I start my day at five a.m. In the quiet house, I find ways to ease my heart. Whatever the season, I write three pages in my journal, then light prayer candles, sending thoughts of hope to those living with pain, loss and injustice.

After this ritual, I take a two-mile walk, often using an indoor video program. Exercise connects body, mind, and spirit. And my friend Beth and I take our walking seriously.

It all began in the summer of 2002. Tired of my health issues, I used Tolkien's trilogy as inspiration to get the exercise done by writing the *LOTR Heath and Fitness Plan*. Beth and I slogged through the "fat marshes" under "heavy orc attacks".

We stepped weekly on our scales for a "Wednesday Warg Weigh-In". We remained strong companions, holding true to one another, through the "Battle of Waist Deep".

Since our college days, when I'd introduced Beth to her future husband, Brien, we'd forged a steadfast friendship. We were in each other's weddings and remained close over three decades.

The last coffee dribbles into my cup, and I add cream and sugar.

Worries will always be there, but with strong family and long-time friends, the hard places of the world can be shared. And fond memories of good times together will keep things in perspective — especially fun recollections such as discussions of Tolkien's works and heated debates of Middle-earth timelines and character lineage! Tolkien's trilogy lives, as does fellowship, through all life's challenges.

I snap the cover on the travel mug and head for the coat closet.

When Grant shared *The Lord of the Rings* with me, it touched my life. The epic tale of good and evil, courageous acts and unfailing love of friendship, gives hope and strength through difficult times and encouragement to celebrate everyday joys.

I grab my purse and coffee and go out the door. Easing my car out of the driveway, I move onto "the road that goes ever on."

Biography: Gwendolyn Van Hout Knechtel. Born to Brunhilde and E. Remy Van Hout, Gwendolyn lived happily in Jakarta, Indonesia with sister Suzanna, until four years later when political unrest moved family to the Netherlands. From there, the four immigrated to the United States to Corvallis, Oregon, and then to Des Moines, Washington. The close-knit family remains in the Seattle area where, with husbands and children, they cared for their father till the end of his hospice days. The care continues for their mother, recovering from a recent stroke. More than ever, Tolkien's trilogy gives strength through this difficult time for the author.

165

Galadriel's Gift

Laura McMahon

The Lord of the Rings first became part of my reality when I was a teenager, a long time ago. At first, I found it difficult to get into the books, but then it became a grand adventure that I couldn't put down. Tolkien's world seemed so real, as if I could go there if I just tried hard enough. Middle-earth was my refuge, a safe haven to which I could escape. I am now in my early 40's, and my love of the story has only deepened through the years.

When the movies came out, it was a dream come true watching my favorite story come to life on the screen. To see all of my favorite characters, especially Galadriel, was a joy. The films have rekindled my deep yearning to go to Middle-earth, since I'm convinced it does exist somewhere....

But since I have yet to find the way there, I've made it my goal to recreate my favorite places from Middle-earth here, on my own property. To do that, I've been researching different plants and drawing up sketches of gardens and secret places for this future dream world.

I began by focusing on details from the book. I read and re-read anything that could give me insight into the landscapes of Middle-earth. My plan is to re-create the forests of Mirkwood, the gardens of Rivendell and the Golden Wood of Lothlorien. I am concentrating first on the trees, since those are integral parts of at least two of the realms.

One of my best resources has been *Eyewitness Handbook: Trees*, by Allen J. Coombs, who lives in England. I had been looking for specific tree characteristics, mainly a smooth bark for my "mallorns". After a few years of seeking, I thought I had found what I needed. When my local experts were unable to place them from my photos and clippings, I sent them to Mr. Coombs,

166

who identified them as American Beech trees, *Fagus Grandifolia*. The beech tree fits the description of the mallorn almost to a T. I was thrilled. I then focused on the other trees of Lothlorien. I found another tree which seems to suit my criteria, but have been unable to identify it. I may be contacting Mr. Coombs for help again!

I am still looking for gold and white flowers to represent the niphredil and elanor of Lothlorien. No one seems to have any clues for me, but I don't give up easily. Since I haven't been able to find my beech trees in any nurseries, I am trying to root cuttings and grow them into saplings for planting in my "mallorn" grove. I would like to add a large water feature resembling a creek with an elven bridge, or a large pond with an elven 'dock" on it. If I can find the proper trees, I also plan to re-create the ring of trees at Cerin Amroth, and place a small tribute to Arwen's passing there. The final touch will be an elven *flet* styled after the ones in *The Fellowship of the Ring*.

Rivendell is a bit easier, since I'm creating a garden of assorted shrubs, flowers, and evergreens. It will definitely have a water feature. I have also sketched out plans for an elven gazebo. For Mirkwood, I've started a grove of assorted evergreens, including white pines, loblolly pines, and Leland's cypresses, and will be adding some cedars to make an interesting mix. Then I'll put in benches for reading and relaxing under the whispering pines. It will be a real woodland wonderland. My goal is to make you feel as if you are really there, in Middle-earth.

All this research and planning has been my lifeline over the past few years, which have been particularly stressful and overwhelming. Whenever I need solace, I retreat to Middle-earth and my future re-creation of it. I hope many others will find a safe haven in Middle-earth as I have.

Biography: Laura McMahon. "I was born in Houston, Texas in 1962 and read *The Hobbit* and *The Lord of the Rings* when I was just twelve years old. At first I had a hard time with the names, but once I got past that things really picked up. I fell in love with the story and couldn't put it down. *The Fellowship of the Ring* was my favorite book; I wanted to go to Lothlorien and meet Galadriel and Celeborn. *I still do!* I couldn't wait to see what my favorite characters looked like in the movie. I have also read *The Silmarillion* and all the other books I could find relating to Middle-earth and its history. As you can see, I can't get enough of Tolkien's world.

Middle-earth has become my alternate reality. I'm now 43 and intend to pass this treasure along to my children and grandchildren. Thanks to Middle-earth I will always be young at heart. *Namarië!*"

Galadriel's Helper

Lembas for the Soul

Quest for the Lost Road
Catherine Kohman

Because of my decision to publish *Lembas for the Soul*, I've made many new friends, both online and in person. The book also gave me the perfect excuse to attend two recent Tolkien conferences: the Marquette University conference in the fall of 2004 and *Tolkien 2005* in Birmingham, England. The last time I was in the UK was back in 1985. I've always thought of the West Country as a second home, and it felt wonderful to be in England again.

My friend Julie also came to "Brum", and we had a great time at the conference, shopping in the city and enjoying the fantastic Indian food. I connected with Lynnette Porter and Brenda Tuttle, both *Lembas for the Soul* authors, which was fun. In addition to listening to all the illuminating presentations, I met Tolkien illustrator and conceptual *LOTR* film artist Alan Lee. He kindly and patiently answered my questions about his forthcoming work. The fellowship and camaraderie at both conferences was amazing. It would be hard to find another group of people who are as bright, witty and genuinely good-hearted as *Lord of the Rings* fans.

After the Birmingham conference, Kathy, a friend I'd met at Marquette, and I made a Midlands pilgrimage to sites associated with Tolkien and Middle-earth. We started in Birmingham, the city of Tolkien's youth, and visited Sarehole Mill, the basis for Sandyman's mill in *LOTR*, and Moseley Bog, where Tolkien and his brother played as children. This dark and mysterious forest, which supposedly was a model for The Old Forest, is now part of

169

the planned Shire County Park. Members of the local Tolkien group stage dramatizations in the park every May for the thousands of people who attend the festival.

But that was just the start. We stopped at an ancient pub in Nottingham where Professor Tolkien and a colleague once spent a convivial afternoon. *The Trip to Jerusalem* pub is one of the oldest in England, and is carved out of the rock at the base of Nottingham Castle. It has its share of haunted secrets and is a fair place to raise a glass in the Professor's honor.

We visited The White Horse of Uffington, an ancient chalk figure on the North Downs, which could have been Tolkien's inspiration for the banner of Rohan. When I stood atop White Horse Hill, I imagined I was on the terrace at Meduseld. The wind carved scrolling patterns on the grass and wheat fields below, and on the horizon I could almost see three distant figures on horseback approaching the foot of the downs. Later that afternoon as we drove through the surrounding countryside, we saw hills and villages that could be twins of Tolkien's drawing of The Hill and Hobbiton. We were seeing the landscape anew through the eyes of someone who knew Middle-earth well.

When we came to Oxford, we spent the entire day walking the streets of that golden dream of a city, tracing Tolkien's footsteps, from his Colleges, to the Radcliffe Camera and the Bodleian Library. I felt I was breathing rarefied air as I climbed those same hallowed stairs and peeked into the stacks of the venerable Duke Humphrey's Library. And no visit to Oxford would be complete without a stop at *The Eagle and The Child* pub. On a quiet, sunny afternoon, Kathy and I lunched in the Inklings' favorite room and soaked up the rich literary atmosphere.

At the end of the long day, we stopped in Northmoor Road to see two of Tolkien's homes, and then headed to Wolvercote Cemetery. As the shadows gathered, we found the grave where Tolkien and his beloved wife Edith are buried, beneath a headstone that also bears the names of Beren and Luthien. The grave was covered with mementos: flowers, a few rosaries, personal notes and odd trinkets. One of the most touching was a toy eagle. Among the last summer roses, someone had planted a rosemary bush ... *rosemary for remembrance*, I thought. The cemetery caretakers warned us they'd soon be closing the gate, and as we paid one last silent tribute to the Professor, tears filled our eyes. The pilgrimage was over.

We turned for one last look. Framed between two tall cedars, the setting sun gilded a jet trail. As I gazed up at the long streak of molten gold arcing over the Professor's grave, I said, "Look — it's Eärendil crossing the evening sky." I laughed through my tears. "Perhaps it's a sign ... Middle-earth really exists. All we have to do is find *The Lost Road*."

As Quests go, it's a wondrous journey, a path we are all bound — by love — to take.

May the light of Eärendil shine upon us all!

Celevon*, the Tenth Walker

Biography: Catherine Kohman. A life-long fan of *The Lord of the Rings*, Catherine Kohman has seen her Tolkien book collection grow from just *The Hobbit* and *LOTR* to an entire bookshelf groaning under the weight of all her Tolkien-related titles. Her first novel, *The Beckoning Ghost*, won the *Golden Heart Award* from Romance Writers of America. She is currently working on a light, comic mystery set in the Southwest and an original fantasy novel. Her website is www.whitetreepress.com.

Catherine lives with her husband in a pastoral woodland setting she likes to envision as part of the Shire. They share their home with three rescued sighthounds: two whippets and a former racing greyhound who doesn't seem to know he's retired.

She hopes that by the time she saves enough money for a trip to New Zealand, Peter Jackson will be filming *The Hobbit*. She has first dibs on the job of passing out snacks to the cast and crew.

*No, it's not a mistake; it's a pun — in Elvish.

The Time That is Given to Us
Linda Turner

On September 11, 2001, I was at home and saw the tragic events unfold on live TV. Since I live in central Maryland, I was in the midst of all the fear and turmoil, and the terrorist attacks deeply affected me. At the time, I was employed at a company that dealt with pilots. For days after the attacks, I was subjected to the outraged rants of private pilots who were temporarily grounded. They seemed not to care in the least about what had just happened and were angry that their expensive hobby had been put on hold for a few days. I was both angered and saddened by their self-centered arrogance. I spent the next few months in a fog of bitterness, confusion, and sadness that nothing seemed to penetrate.

Just four months later, I sat in a darkened theater watching *The Fellowship of the Ring*. I had read the books a couple of times over the years, so I was familiar with the story. My daughter had given me tickets for the movie as a Christmas gift. So I sat, lost in the fantasy of the movie, when Gandalf and Frodo had their talk in the mines of Moria. Frodo said how he wished none of this had happened in his lifetime. Something tingled in my mind. The fog shimmered. Gandalf responded that all we had to decide was what to do with the time that was given to us. A lightening bolt struck inside of me, the fog lifted and I knew at that instant my life was changed.

All of those people who had died in the attacks on 9/11 thought they had all the time in the world. They were mostly young, rising professionals. There would be time to travel, time to relax, time to go after their dreams *later*. Right now, their

172

work was the most important thing: working overtime, getting those reports done, earning the money so that *later* they could enjoy themselves. Later didn't come. Those oh-so-important reports were nothing but ashes and confetti raining down and no one was going to miss them. They weren't going to matter after all. "Decide what to do with the time that is given to us."

I was 46 at the time. My two children were 14 and 19. I was acutely aware that tomorrow might not be there for me either. "Wait until the kids are gone." "Wait until we retire." Not now. It was time to start living our dreams.

The first thing I did was to book a trip to New Zealand. I *had* to go. My husband was more than willing to go along. It would involve camping, hiking, and glacier climbing, and would be a real adventure trip. I had been a beach person most of my life, but I felt a backpacker emerging. The beach bum was slowly giving way. I found an enthusiasm for the outdoors I didn't know was there. My husband was astounded at the change. I started working out, walking miles and miles on the treadmill and on trails. And all the while I pictured the Fellowship trekking its way along, no matter how hard the going was.

I applied for the time off from work — three weeks — that I'd need for the trip and was turned down. I quit my job. This was far too important. I bought backpacking equipment, magazines and books. The things I had taken pleasure in before, like "ladies" magazines on gardening and decorating, suddenly seemed incredibly shallow to me, and I was horrified I had wasted so much time on them. I signed us up for our cable TV provider's digital cable programming so we could watch *The National Geographic Channel* and *The Travel Channel*.

I was laughing more and friends were telling me I was a different person, a happier person, than they'd seen in several months. I found myself dressing for the outdoors and tossing out the pantyhose and heels. I was so much more comfortable with myself. Out went all of my Jimmy Buffet CDs and in came Enya with her peaceful, contemplative music. I haunted eBay for *The Lord of the Rings* and Tolkien items, starting a collection of his works and anything related to him.

173

By the time the second movie premiered, we were just two months away from our New Zealand trip. I was in terrific shape and filled with a sense of adventure I'd never known before. We arrived in Auckland in February 2003, and were immediately in love with New Zealand. On a day-long bus tour of the North Island, the bus driver played a DVD — it was *The Fellowship of the Ring*. I had the most surreal experience while watching the movie and then looking out the bus window to see the same scenery going by. Tears started pouring down. I had made it. *I was in Middle-earth.*

Our tour group set out a couple of days later. It was made up of three Aussies in their 20's, an American woman in her 30's, and a South African woman also in her 30's. We were the oldest by more than ten years. But we all shared a love of *LOTR* and the young Kiwi woman who was our guide made sure we took the occasional side trip to see filming locations. I was by far the most avid fan of the group and would get positively giddy when standing where Arwen and Frodo raced to the Ford, walking down the river to the Ford itself, hiking up the scree-covered mountainside of Mount Ruapehu where Sam and Frodo realized they were "going in circles" and met up with Gollum.

Our hostel had an amazing view of Mount Tongariro — "Mount Doom" in the movies. We drove through the primeval forest land of Glenorchy, filming location both for Lothlorien and Orthanc. And we arrived in Wellington just days before *The Lord of the Rings*: Special Exhibit closed at the Te Papa Museum. I was mesmerized as I slowly made my way through the room filled with the swords, costumes, jewelry, banners, and even the elven canoe with a very life-like Boromir in it in his repose of death.

On the day we climbed Fox Glacier, we all decided to pose for a group picture on top of a huge boulder. Being the shortest one — I'm only 4'10" — and the group's Official Hobbit, I had to reach for a hand up. As she reached to help me, 20-year-old Erica from Australia said, "Come on, Mrs. Baggins." The name stuck. It is now my "trail name" on the Appalachian Trail and is my screen name for *theOneRing.net* message boards, as well as in the local fan group to which I belong. It appears on my nametags at the Moots I've attended for the *LOTR* Symphonies. I cherish it as the "other me" that takes over and forges ahead whenever I am fearful or hesitant.

When it was nearing time for the final movie, I went to *theOneRing.net* and tried to get a line party started in my town. One person responded, amazed that anyone else in our town was a Ringer. We exchanged e-mails. I told her I was going to be interviewed by our local paper about my collection of *LOTR* items and my trip to New Zealand. Would she like to be a part of it?

She was thrilled and we met the day before the interview. We had so much in common and talked like old friends for three hours. Her collection dwarfed my own and she was so knowledgeable about the movies and the books. She in turn got me a ticket to Trilogy Tuesday when someone in her group backed out. At that event I met several other women who were devoted to all things *LOTR*. They formed a group known as The Other Nine and I was accepted into it as the tenth member. Several of us attended the Atlanta Moot and *LOTR* Symphony together.

I'm 49 now. I've been to the Chicago Moot and Symphony. I've had the privilege of meeting and speaking with both Alan Lee and the late Karen Wynn Fonstad twice and getting their autographs. I've also been on adventure trips to Ireland, England and Guatemala. My closet is lined with travel gear and trekking clothing. I don't even own a suitcase now — just backpacks and daypacks.

My collection of *LOTR* and Tolkien items has grown so much I've had to purchase display cases for it all. While in New Zealand, I bought a replica of The One Ring and wear it every day. I take great comfort in it and when I find myself afraid to do something, I look at it, let Mrs. Baggins emerge, and forge ahead.

Last year, I got my first tattoo. My daughter's reaction? "Oh my God, Mom, I hope it's not some hobbit thing!" No, it's a sunburst, but I'm thinking about adding "some hobbit thing" to it! We adopted a kitten and I named him Pippin.

I'm getting used to the eye rolling and completely mystified looks I get from friends and family about it all. They will never understand the strength and joy it has brought me, the determination to live out my dreams that has been wrought within me. "All we have to decide is what to do with the time that is given to us." I have decided to spend it dedicated to the 3000 people who lost their lives on 9/11, as if every day were the last. It may well be.

Biography: Linda Turner. "I've been married for 30 years to my high school sweetheart, Tim. We have two kids, Sarah, 23, and Adam, 18. I was born in California, have lived in nine states, Germany (Berlin, before the Wall came down), and have traveled to most of Western Europe as well as Ireland, the UK, New Zealand, Australia, Guatemala, Mexico, 46 of the 50 states, and the Bahamas. I currently live in Maryland. I've hiked sections of the Appalachian Trail. My interest in J.R.R. Tolkien has led me to visit his grave in England and to study the writings of C.S. Lewis."

Lembas For the Soul

Catherine Kohman's books are available at finer bookstores around the world or via the Internet at Whitetreepress.com and at Amazon.com.

For more information about J.R.R. Tolkien and his works, please visit the following websites:

The Tolkien Society

www.tolkiensociety.org

The Tolkien Society has chapters or "smials" all over the world and publishes the journal Amon Hen. They hold an annual get-together called "Oxonmoot" every September in Oxford, England.

theOneRing.net

Serving Middle-earth since the First Age

The latest news of LOTR film, book publishing and related events. They also sponsor ORC, the One Ring Celebration, usually held in January in southern California.

The Council of Elrond

www.councilofelrond.com

A wealth of LOTR information and images of Middle-earth.

Winner of *The Golden Heart Award*

The Beckoning Ghost

By Catherine Kohman

The ghost of dashing explorer Brendan Tyrell haunts Marissa Erickson, his biographer. Their meeting stirs up dangerous currents from the past as well as unsolved mysteries.

"An engrossing mix of history, mystery and what might be..." — **Tami Hoag**, NY Times Bestselling Author.

"Five Stars!" — **Holly Damiano**, *Affaire De Coeur.*

"Great hero, great book!" — **Kristin Ramsdell**, co-author of *What Do I Read Next?*

Available at
www.whitetreepress.com

Also watch for her forthcoming book,

Groom Upgrade

Phaedra Kendall thinks nothing could be worse than getting dumped on her honeymoon. She may be wrong...*dead* wrong.

3577569R00101

Printed in Great Britain
by Amazon.co.uk, Ltd.,
Marston Gate.